ANN DENTON

LE RUE PUBLISHING

Le Rue Publishing
320 South Boston Avenue, Suite 1030
Tulsa, OK 74103
www.LeRuePublishing.com

ISBN: 978-1-7335960-4-6

To Mary Jo. Hope you enjoy.

CHAPTER ONE

Heather bursts into the exam room just as Doc Stife is about to pull a tooth. His pliers are literally poised over old Mrs. Jones's mouth and I'm wetting her tongue with the water syringe and suctioning the spit out with my trusty saliva ejector.

"Holy motherfucking shit!" Heather yells. Really loud.

I jump and accidentally spray the old woman with the water syringe and simultaneously choke her with the suction tube. "Crap, sorry, Mrs. Jones! Sorry, sorry,"

I yank the saliva ejector tube back and grab a paper towel from the stack on the instrument table so that I can mop up the old woman's face. I pat her down as I whisper more apologies. She's gonna hate me. Doc Stife probably already hates me.

Dammit Heather!

Heather grabs my hand with her manicured claw and yanks me away from Mrs. Jones before I can swipe the water puddled in the hollow of the poor woman's neck. Heather stares right at my boss and says—in her Okie accent, "Sorry, Stife, family emergency. Katie's gotta go now!"

My stomach turns to jelly. What is she doing? She's gonna get me fired! My eyes flit to my grey-haired boss, pleading with him not to take this out on me.

Stife shakes his head at Heather, not even glancing my way. His deep voice grumbles, "She can't—"

Heather does not listen to the good doctor. She yanks my hand harder and that accidentally pulls the water tube out of the machine because it was still in my hand. Water splatters from the tube to the floor, puddling near Doc's leather shoes.

Dammit.

I'm gonna be the one that has to clean that up.

"Heather—" I try to keep my tone from whining. Or screeching. But I kinda want to shake her and say, 'Save the drama for afterhours!' Of course, she wouldn't. She's Heather. She does what she wants. Including interrupting us mid-dental procedure for the fourth "family emergency" in six months.

This better not be like the last family emergency Heather had, where her cat Zeebo was lost for four hours and showed up the same frickin' night, looking all self-satis-fied and well-sexed. I spent hours crawling under bushes at Zinc Park that day. Zeebo's a dick.

But then again, so is his mom.

I had to lie about that one. I wrack my brain to remember what I said, in case this is another crap emergency. I eye Doc Stife as I think.

My boss is in shock, his wrinkled forehead folded up with double the lines he normally has. He's experienced Heather's emergencies before—obviously, because she'd never have an emergency without running to get me—but never mid-surgery.

Doc Stife looks torn between yelling at her to get out and just sighing and letting me go. Heather's not an easy one to convince to back down. Besides being 5'8" and too pretty for most people to ever be honest with her, she's got the mouth of a shark. As in, she rips people to bits. She once told off an entire boys' soccer team on my behalf in high school. But that's why she's my main gal. My ride or die. I'd rather face a shark than tell Stife to give me a raise. Heather's gotten my last two raises for me via public shaming. Once in the lobby. Once online. (Stife hated that one.)

Stife looks to me for confirmation that this is actually an emergency-emergency and not just a Heather-emer-gency. I stare at Heather. Because I have no clue. Since her divorce finalized last month, it's getting harder to tell.

Her mermaid hair is in disarray. (Heather's hair is never in disarray. Her hair is her art piece. She can literally make those crazy-ass roses out of hair.) Her blue eyes are wild and the liner on them is smudged. Something bad must have happened if my supermodel-wannabe hairstylist bestie is looking this unkempt in public. Something super bad. Fuck.

I think this is a real emergency.

I bite my lip, worry starting to gather in my stomach, like a rising tide, ready to wash over me as soon as she drops the news. "Is it my mom?"

"Nope."

"My dad?" My parents are the closest thing to parents she has, so I ask about them first.

"Nope."

"Ms. Michaels, is this an actual emergency? Involving humans?" Stife loses his patience as he dabs angrily at the water splashed all over our patient's neck. Mrs. Jones gags a bit when he presses too hard, but he doesn't seem to notice.

My heart thumps faster as I realize the implications of what Stife just said. My eyes widen. I definitely did not tell him about the lost cat. Which means one of the girls at work did.

Mrs. Jones (whose mouth is currently stretched with a dental lip retractor so that she looks like a porn-star caught in freeze frame in that moment after a blow job) gargles frantically and pulls at the doc's sleeve.

Stife pats the woman's arm absently, but his eyes stay on Heather.

"Katie's about to help with a procedure."

Yup. That's true. I was. But now my foot is sliding toward the door. I'd never take on the boss directly. But I'm feeling the panic. The anxiety. I really do believe Heather this time. That something's wrong. But if I leave, Stife's gonna be pissed at me. I hate when anyone's mad at me. Fuck.

Heather tosses her green and blue mermaid locks proudly. "You'll have to get someone else. Katie has to leave."

My knees start to shake a little. Heather's tone is so firm it brooks no argument. Aw, shit. It's one of my sisters. I just know it. I'm the oldest of four. "Is it—"

Heather cuts me off, knowing what I'm gonna ask. "Nope. Not your sisters."

"What is this emergency?" Stife asks, ignoring Mrs. Jones, who's sat up and is tugging at the retractor, trying to pry it off her mouth.

Heather's eyes narrow, "I already said it's a family emergency. And I don't think HIPPA would like to know you were buttin' in to—"

"HIPPA is only for medical issues—"

"Did I say it *wasn't* medical?" Heather leans forward and her eyes get wide and aggressive.

Stife's jaw ticks. Shit's about to go down. They both look pissed as all get out and all I want to do is hide under the instrument table. Why can't everybody just act like grown ups?

At that very moment, Mrs. Jones heaves and an involuntary spit projectile smacks Stife's face. Most of it splatters across his glasses, but some of it lands on his cheek and slides down his face, a thick yellow glob.

It's the final straw. The pulse in his neck throbs.

Panic shoots through me. I can't stand the tension. It feels like I'm burning, shoved into a fire. I have to try to put out the flames. I speak slowly and quietly—like I'm talking to an injured animal, "Doc Stife, I'll just help her for a sec and be right back. I'll get all this cleaned up and then we can finish ..." I nod encouragingly at him.

Heather stops my attempt at peacemaking with one line. "She won't be back." She grabs my hand and yanks me toward the door. "Sorry. You're gonna need a new assistant." Heather rips off my lab coat and tosses it at Stife.

Fuck! I frantically shake my head at Doctor Stife. "She's kidding!" I call over my shoulder as I'm dragged down the hallway past co-workers and small children who cry as they are led toward the teeth-brushing station.

Heather grits out, "Oh, I'm not joking, Katie. You're done here."

She pulls me into the parking lot. It's mid-afternoon and it's bright as fuck. At least today is somewhat warm. Spring in Oklahoma has Heather's temperament: unpredictable. I squint in the light and pull my brown hair out of its standard low ponytail.

"What the hell, Feather?" I only call her that when I'm pissed, because she hates it. But she just tried to make me quit my fucking job. J-O-B. The one thing I've been able to hold together since high school. "You don't get to decide what I quit."

Heather raises her eyebrows. "Smoking."

"That was bad for me."

"Jeremy."

"He was bad for me."

"Those god-awful purple pants with the flowers on them."

I clench my fists. "Those had nothing to do with you. They got a stain on them."

"I spilled red jam on them on purpose."

Those were my favorite pants! "Are you trying to get me to punch you?"

Heather laughs. She scoops me into the biggest hug in the world, ignoring my spit-stained scrubs. "You're quittin', Katie. And you're never going back again."

I shake my head and pull out of the hug. "Are you crazy? Did you take something?"

Heather throws her head back and laughs. She digs through her purse.

Instantly, I grow suspicious. "Are you on cold medicine?" Last time she took cold medicine, she went fucking psycho. Hilariously psycho. She babbled about all kinds of shit. Called her ex's dick a sweet pickle. But that time, she wasn't walking into my office and quitting my job for me.

"No, I'm not on cold medicine, loser," she scoffs.

"Then what the fuck?"

She grabs something out of her purse and starts waving it in the air. Whatever it is, a crumpled napkin or something, flies out of her hand and onto the asphalt.

"Fucking fuck!" she dives after the piece of trash like it's some damned priceless diamond or something.

The wind rolls the little paper under her car and I watch Heather lay full out on the black top and grunt and squeeze herself as far under the car as she can, ruining her manicure scraping at the ground. Finally, she grabs hold of the post-it and wiggles out. She stands and holds up her treasure triumphantly. "Yes," she breathes, like she's some freaking killer in a horror movie.

I take a step back. My mom has always called Heather crazy. I've never agreed. But right in this moment, I'm questioning my own judgment.

"What is wrong with you?" I ask.

Heather unwrinkles her little orange paper square and holds it up. She walks slowly toward me, both hands holding the it securely. "You are never gonna go back to that crap job again, Katie. Cuz' I just won the mother-fuckin' lotto."

"No."

"Yup. Read it and weep, biotch!"

I grab the little sheet of paper and look over the numbers.

Heather grabs her old phone from her purse and shoves it under my nose. She has the lotto site all pulled up.

My eyes flit from phone to paper. Phone to paper and back again. "Are you sure?"

"Yes!" She freaks and snatches the phone and paper out of my hands to check them over again herself. "I checked like twenty times last night. Called your phone. You didn't answer."

I bite my lip. I don't tell her I was with Jeremy last night. No need to argue about him.

She scans the numbers a third time. "They totally match!"

I clear my throat. I—unlike Heather—don't like to stir the shit. But this is the most crazy/serious thing she's every claimed. "But, like, did you make sure they're from the same day? You know, sometimes that website is slow to update." It would be the worst if she went into the lotto office and got all embarrassed because she looked at numbers from the wrong day. My cheeks heat up just thinking about it.

Heather scrolls on her phone and then shoves in under my nose. "There!"

The date is yesterday.

She holds up the ticket. The date matches.

My jaw unhinges, falls to the ground, and rolls away. Somehow, I still manage to talk. Maybe it's a miracle. Because crazy-ass miracles are happening here. "Holy motherfucking shit, Heather!" My brown eyes meet her blue ones. Shock meets smug.

She tosses her mermaid hair with pride, as though this is some accomplishment and not stupid luck. "I know, right?"

I grab her phone and scroll through the site. "What was the pot?"

"Two-hundred fifty-two million. Cash value: the site says one-hundred fifty-three."

I drop the phone. My scream sends people from my office pouring out into the parking lot. Even Doc Stife. Rubber-necking is an Olympic sport in Oklahoma.

A crowd starts approaching. I start panicking. "Crap. We can't tell them. All those TV shows say you can't tell anyone. They'll all beg you for money."

Heather holds up a hand to the crowd. "I've got chlamy-dia! Get back inside!"

When my office sees it's just me screaming ... and just Heather causing the screaming, and she's claiming she has STDs, they actually listen. Probably because it's better than confronting Heather head on. Doing that would be like running straight at a moving combine harvester. Or some death robot—the kind with rotating blades for hands. Basically, the same metaphor. She's sharp and nasty and scary as fuck. And she just became a motherfucking millionaire

CHAPTER TWO

I sit down at family dinner and keep my hands clasped in my lap. I learned a long time ago that avoiding eye contact with my mother is the easiest way to avoid confrontation.

I stare down at our chipped plates as mom brings out dishes from the kitchen for dinner. Carrots, cheesy cabbage, hot corn ... she goes back and forth for each dish, long ago having refused to let any of us help. She might serve the food, but Mom runs our family. She's the alpha, the pant-wearer, the big kahoona. And I'm pretty sure she's gonna want to bite my head off if she finds out I've quit my job.

I made it official with a margarita-brave email to Doc Stife this afternoon. I'd never loved working for him. But the recession had hit, and all the party-planning companies I'd applied for had shriveled up and blown away faster than you can say dandelion fuzz. So, I'd stayed.

Pretty sure Mom'll go nuclear if she ever finds out I flat-out refused to take a cool mil off Heather, too. But I will not be some leech who just hangs around her for her money. She'd laughed when I said that earlier.

I'd simply shaken my head. "I've watched enough of those 'The Lotto Ruined Me' shows. Too many people only come or stick around for the cash. I won't be one of those."

"Fine, then take a loan. Start that party-planning company you've always wanted," Heather had sniffed, offended that I wouldn't let her trot off to the bank and get hundred-dollar bills to toss at me so I could roll around in them like some movie star.

"A loan?" I'd stared at her long and hard. Hope had filled me. Visions of weddings, of smiling people, of beautiful banquet tables had danced like sugarplums through my head. I'd helped my extended family with their events for years. Run at least a dozen weddings. I always loved seeing the smiles on people's faces during the ceremony, knowing I'd helped. But a loan? The worried side of my mind had whispered that mixing money and friendship was a bad idea. Someone was bound to get hurt.

"I can see that look. You're talking yourself out of it. Don't. I'll make this all official. A business transaction. We'll get a lawyer to draw up the paperwork and everything."

My voice had wavered as the two sides of me warred with

each other. Dreams. Friendship. Dreams. Friendship. "What if I fail?"

She'd grabbed my hand, nearly knocking over our margaritas. "Then at least you tried." Her blue eyes were calm and steady and sure. As always, Heather's determination was like a blowtorch burning away my resistance. "Come on, now. It's not like the money you need will make a dent in what I'm getting."

I'd caved. I'd nodded. "I'll try."

Her self-satisfied smirk hadn't done a damn thing to quell my excitement. Nope. This afternoon I'd been as excited as the day Bobby Lee asked me to the ninth-grade dance. Heather had pushed and bought me margaritas until I'd sent that tipsy resignation email.

I smile as I think about her. I hope she's not getting up to trouble right now. She'd gone and bought herself a new phone and a tablet so she could do some online shopping tonight. I mutter to myself, "She's probably buying fucking bamboo toilet paper—"

"Bamboo toilet paper?" My sister, Olivia, pulls up a chair next to me. Olivia is a mechanic, normally covered in oil stains and wearing a ponytail at the nape of her neck. But not in my mother's house. Nope. In here, she isn't even a closet lesbian. She's Irma Jean's straight-A, straight-backed daughter with a button up shirt and freshly ironed slacks.

My car-wrinkled black maxi dress doesn't compare. I self-consciously smooth out the wrinkles as Olivia smiles at me and sits. We look a bit alike, with the brown hair and eyes and straight brows. But she's definitely got a hard edge to her. And she's a couple inches taller than me. She's also way more sure of herself than I've ever been.

"Is bamboo toilet paper really a thing?" Olivia asks.

I roll my eyes. "Apparently. Heather saw it on some show. It's expensive as all get out and supposed to be like wiping with a cloud. She's obsessed with it."

"Of course, she is," Olivia chuckles. "When you're that big of an asshole, you need a gentle wipe."

My dad actually snickers from his seat.

My mother calls out from the kitchen. "You cursing in my house, Katie Ann?"

I call out, "No ma'am."

"You lying, too?"

"It was Olivia!"

My sister pipes up and yells over me, "Was not!"

"Was too!"

My mother hip checks the door and walks in with a heaping platter of fried chicken and baloney. My mouth starts to water.

Mom gives me the stink eye. "You feeling rebellious today?"

"No ma'am." I stare at the table. I learned a long time ago not to look to my dad for help. He'll just sit there and let Mom dole out whatever she wants. Usually, it's a big steaming helping of criticism.

Mom gives me a stare but then goes back into the kitchen to bring out something else.

Olivia leans into me and whispers, "Heads up, she knows. Sophie heard."

Bile seeps into my throat. My stomach starts to churn as my mother brings in a bowl of mashed potatoes. My gaze flickers toward her against my will, and I see a fiery gleam in mom's eyes.

I might be thirty, but I slink down in my chair like a six-year-old when I see that look.

"Dad, I might need to go outside to get a breath of fresh air."

My dad looks up from his tablet and raises his eyebrows. "Katie, it's a hundred degrees out there with seventy-five percent humidity right now." He takes a swig from his glass of whiskey. Ice cubes clink in the glass as I bite my lip and try to think of some justification for going outside into the Jurassic Period weather that is an Oklahoman evening.

I look at Olivia and beg her with my eyes to help me out. She just shrugs and takes another sip of her sweet tea.

"You ratted me out about the cursing. I'm being pretty generous with the heads up."

I lean closer and whisper to her, "What exactly has mom heard?"

"What exactly are you worried I've heard young lady?" My mother's voice comes from directly behind me.

I freeze in my seat, my limbs locked up like one of those stupid fainting goats. Fuck. She must've gone around through the kitchen into the living room so she could attack from behind.

My mom strolls around the table and stands behind her chair. She eyes me like some megalomaniac CEO. Or the devil about to decide which layer of hell to send me to.

When I don't answer, she picks at her bright red nails and says casually, "Your other two sisters couldn't make it tonight. Sophie had a volleyball game, and Charlotte is *working*."

There it is. The dig. I cringe. She knows. She knows Heather pulled me out of work today and that I didn't go back. I briefly wonder if she's hacked my email. But Mom doesn't do technology.

I glance over at Dad. He's still swiping through his tablet. Oblivious. I'm gonna hazard a guess it he didn't hack my email unless she threatened to take his whiskey away.

I give Mom a weak smile. "How's Sophie's team doing?"

My mother takes her seat and smooths her skirt, folding her hands on the table. "Let's say grace first."

My father puts down his tablet and takes one more drink as if he needs it to get through prayer. He thinks he needs it to get through life in general, so why would prayer be any different?

I fold my hands and bow my head. God, please let me make it through this dinner without getting my head bitten off and without spilling the beans. My mother does not need to know Heather won the lotto.

Heather might be able to stand up to the woman—she started telling her off when we were twelve and got in trouble for wearing an inappropriate shade of lipstick—but I sure as hell can't. Mom would ban me from the family. Dad, I could live without. He's not a bad guy, but he's about as useful as a screen door on a submarine. But the girls? Mom would never let my sisters talk to me again. Olivia might rebel and still talk to me on the down low, but the others? They're young. Less defiant, like me.

Mom wraps up grace and passes around some fried chicken and fried baloney. "I saw Mrs. Casem today."

I can tell by her tone that this is the lead in to my doom. So, I simply swallow the ping-pong ball stuck in my throat and say, "Mmhmm."

"She's friends with a woman named Francine, who was at your office today. Apparently, Francine was about to have some work done when—and I quote, 'Some blue-haired hussy burst in and dragged off the dental assistant.'" Mom stares pointedly at me, her brown eyes as dark and dangerous as quicksand.

I trace old scratch marks on the dining table. "It wasn't exactly like that."

"What was it like?"

"Heather had an emergency," I say weakly.

My shoulders collapse in a little further. For some reason, being at my mother's house always makes me feel like I'm on the verge of being sent to my room. Maybe because I spent a good chunk of my childhood there, or else with my nose in the corner. I couldn't put a toe out of line without her cracking the whip.

My mother's never been one for 'shenanigans' as she calls them. Heather's always been a master at shenanigans. It's probably why I fell into bestie love with her at first sight when I was six years old and we moved into this house. She was three days from turning seven and had been climbing up the gutter on her house to reach a Frisbee stuck on her roof. She hadn't even screamed when she'd fallen and broken her arm. I'd thought she was the bravest kid I ever met as we drove her to the ER because her own parents weren't home.

"Heather," Mom shakes her head. "That girl is a living, breathing emergency. She should come with flashing lights and a siren so you can get out of the way," my mother rolls her eyes as she serves the carrots. "Homer, you haven't put salad on your plate." She pushes the salad bowl back toward my father. Mom's a real multi-tasking nagger. She can juggle nagging all five of us at once.

Her eyes flick back to me. "Why did Francine tell Mrs. Casem that you walked out and quit your job?"

I can feel the blush take over my cheeks unbidden. Fucking fuck. For whatever reason, I didn't figure mom would find out the same day. I thought I'd have awhile to think of something reasonable. Something that was not a lotto win. Of course, she'd find out though, it's Tulsa—god-damned biggest small town there ever was. Shocking news travels faster than a lightning bolt. Shit. I chew my lip and glance at Olivia.

My sister shrugs. There's not much she can do to save me.

Mom sniffs, "If you think for one second, you're gonna move back in here—"

"I'm not." I'm just as horrified by that thought as she looks.

"What in God's good name were you thinking? Quitting a decent job—"

"I'm ... starting my own business?" It comes out as a question.

Mother narrows her eyes. "And how are you gonna pull that off?"

I gulp. "I ... got a loan."

My father chimes in for once. "A loan? Well, that's awful professional of you, honey."

I nod in thanks.

Mom's not convinced. "A loan for what?"

I rub my lips together, already anticipating her reaction. "An event planning company."

"Event planning? Like weddings?"

I nod and take a bite of hot corn. The jalapeño's too strong and my tongue starts to burn. I take a gulp of water and I nod as tears come to my eyes.

"You know that's not a real job, right? That's a hobby for those women who marry rich men and want to say they do something other than drink mimosas and get manicures all day. There's not real money in that. You planning on getting married? Is there some guy you haven't told me about? I know you hide those men you date from me. Both of you."

Anger boils in the bottom of my stomach. But right beside it is despair. I've always wanted this. Always.

Olivia's hand sneaks under the table to squeeze mine. But she knows better than to start a war with Mom. We can't win.

So, I paste a smile on my face, blink away the tears that I

now have to pretend are solely from the jalepeños, and say, "Dinner's amazing. You've outdone yourself."

My mother sniffs but turns her attention from me to her food. She can't help but have the last word, though. "Mark my words, you're gonna regret this."

Mark my words, Mom. No. I'm not.

CHAPTER THREE

W e've signed papers. It's official. I have a loan for $50,000.00 for my new company, Mark the Moments, LLC. I don't really know why that LLC bit is in there, but lawyers ... they talk, I nod. Things get written down.

But now, I have a little sheet of paper in my purse that says that's the name of my company. Mine. Elation keeps rolling through my stomach. Like pretty little bubbles. It shows up, fills me with wonder, then gets popped by worry the next second. Still, this has to be the best day of my life.

After the loan was done, Heather asked me to stay for other lotto-related, business stuff. I agreed, and we moved from minor loan lawyer's office to the big corner office, where a very serious forty-something man in a dark suit started talking. I agreed to go with Heather, not knowing that all the other money stuff would take hours. Hours. And more hours.

I look at the clock. It's been five hours, to be exact. In five hours, Doc Stife and I could have pulled six teeth. I'm not used to all this sitting still and just jibber jabbering. I have to move. I have to take a break. My head is spinning. I leave the lawyer's office and walk into his reception area.

His big-haired receptionist gives me a sympathetic smile and asks, "Need anything? Coffee? Water?"

I ask for water as I rub my temples. My brain is fried. There are all sorts of legal terms floating around in my head. Living will. Pourover trust. IRA. Investments. All kinds of words I've never had to think about before. Making $13.50 an hour doesn't leave a lotta room for retirement options. It barely leaves enough room for me to decide between a can of green beans or a can of corn at the grocery store. And now Heather's gotta juggle all this crap. It's like walking into a forest and being told, "Go on, hunt your dinner," and being handed a bow and arrow for the first time ever. People with money live in a whole different world.

I envy her, but then again, I don't. Her do-nothing aunt has already hit her up for money. She had to yell at her neighbor and two of her cousins after they saw her name in the local online news and came over trying to get 'loans.' According to the lawyer, that's just the beginning.

Fake relatives will start crawling out of the woodwork looking for handouts.

I sigh.

This lotto shit should be fun. But this lawyer stuff this afternoon is not fun.

"Everything alright?" a sweet tenor voice asks. I glance up to see a walking cream-pie. That's Heather's term for the guys who look so good your panties get wet just by making eye contact.

This guy looks like Barbie's boyfriend. He's got short blond hair swept over to one side. It still sticks up in spots, but in that adorable mussed, just-rolled-out of-bed way that guys can pull off, but no woman can. His eyes are a pale blue. He has some scruff on his face and the scruff has a hint of red in it, which only makes him even hotter, especially since the scruff contrasts the crisp white shirt and ironed pants he's wearing. He has a hint of don't-care on top of his professional, preppy look. The one downside is that he definitely looks younger than me. Shit. Men are only as ripped and in shape as he is in their early twenties. I just turned thirty last week. The yum factor for guys in their thirties goes way down—thanks corporate America for your shitty desk jobs. I finger my brown hair as I eye his pecs.

The hot young dude smirks down at me. Shit. He probably realizes I've been checking him out. I flush with embarrassment and move my eyes from him to the floor.

"Yup, everything's fine," I squeak in answer to the question he asked.

"You look a little flushed," he leans forward, and I smell mint gum. Mint gum triggers a Pavlovian response in me. I automatically think about kissing. It's what my first boyfriend chewed obsessively every time we kissed. Justin even drank mouthwash before he'd see me. He was totally sophomore boy, first-relationship paranoid about having bad breath. My eyes zero in on this hottie's lips. Not too thick, not too thin. Perfectly biteable.

I shake my head, even though I know I'm red as a beet. "It's just overwhelming in there."

"My brother being a dick?" the guy asks.

My eyes fly up and meet his. "That's your brother?" I jerk my head at the lawyer's office. I don't even remember the guy's name in there. Welsh? Walch?

Hot guy extends his hand, "Danny Walsh."

I extend mine. When our fingers touch, a tingle runs through me. I'm not sure if it's my intuition or my lust. All I know is my panties are in for a second round of soaking. Damn. I almost forget to tell Danny my name. "I'm Katie. McPherson. Yup." I cringe. I just said yup. For no fucking reason.

"So, Katie," Danny smiles—it's strange how good my name sounds on his lips, "What are you here for today that's got you so upset?"

I shake my head, "I'm just moral support for a friend. There's just a lot for her to take in."

"Ah," Danny nods knowingly. "Divorce?"

"What? No. Um. Inheritance stuff." That's as close to the truth as I can manage for a stranger. A hot stranger, but still.

"I'm sorry for her loss," Danny says, assuming someone's died. His hand cups my shoulder, encasing it completely. And even though he's just being sympathetic, now my mind is stuck on repeat thinking about how thick his fingers are.

Maybe that's why I don't correct him.

The receptionist walks up at that moment and hands me my water. I think she had to walk to the polar ice caps, chip some ice, melt it, and then come back. That's how long she took. But I don't say anything. It wouldn't do any good. I just smile and take the cup. I take a sip. Luke-warm. Gross.

"I assume you've already had the funeral, but if not, can I suggest an end-of life celebration?" Danny says.

"What's that?"

Danny gestures toward the couch in the reception area and we sit together. He explains, "I work for a company that plans parties and events celebrating someone's life. We could help you. Like, for my aunt, we went to her favorite spot on her running route in tennis shoes. And we all walked the path she normally ran, drinking chai lattes because those were her favorite."

My eyes well up. What a wonderful job. He must be a really thoughtful guy if that's the sorta' work he does. Helping people smile through the pain. "That sounds amazing. The celebration side. But, I'm so sorry about your aunt."

Danny's eyes get a bit misty and he nods, acknowledging me. "She was great. Practically raised me after our parents ..." he trails off.

My hand is on his arm before I can blink. I give a little squeeze. He's an orphan! Just like Heather. Poor sweet thing. "I'm so sorry!"

Danny leans in—

"Danny, are you lying about mom and dad again?" a harsh voice says behind me. The lawyer, Mr. Walsh, glares down at Danny. His glasses have fallen down the bridge of his crooked nose. He crosses his arms and radiates anger down on us.

Beside him, Heather's eyes flicker between Danny and me.

My eyes are on the paunchy lawyer. He and Danny look nothing alike. But then my brain registers what Mr. Walsh said. Lying? My hand snaps back to my stomach. Lying *again*? He said lying again. Like this is a thing.

My eyes fly to Danny. He looks defensive. That must mean it's true.

Danny glares at his brother and stands. "I didn't lie!"

"I heard you talking funerals and acting like they were dead!"

"I never said they were—"

"Of course you didn't. Not outright." The lawyer shakes his salt and pepper head. "Get in my office."

An uncomfortable stare off follows filled with all kinds of facial expressions only family members pull on one another. With their age gap, Lawyer-What's-His-Name Walsh looks like he could almost be Danny's dad. I mean, he could if he'd had Danny when he was like eighteen.

I share a glance with Heather, uncomfortable and a little mortified that I was apparently attracted to a pathological liar. That would be my luck. I've always had the worst taste in guys. Heather's always telling me I should let her pick guys for me instead. She might be fucking right.

Heather comes up next to me and bumps my shoulder with hers. I think she means to be supportive, but I'm just doubly humiliated she saw me cougaring up a liar.

Danny steps toward me. "I wasn't trying to lie—"

"My office," Mr. Walsh says; his voice brooks no argument.

Danny's shoulders sink and he trots off, closing the door quietly behind him.

The attorney sighs and rubs his brow. "I'm sorry. Danny's had issues since he was younger. When he didn't make the Olympics for tennis, everything kind of snowballed. He's been diagnosed as a compulsive liar. He doesn't mean to. But the lies just come out. Often. I'm so sorry about that."

"Does he really work for a party planning place?" I ask.

Mr. Walsh shrugs, "Maybe he did last week. Dunno. Probably not. He goes through jobs like a kid goes through cookies."

Heather's waxed eyebrows shoot up. "So, he's addicted to lying and can't hold down a job?"

She doesn't say it. But I can imagine '*winner*' sarcastically echoing in her head and being telepathically projected at me.

Mr. Walsh shakes his head. "The psychologist said he doesn't have ulterior motives. I think it started as a habit. And he just can't stop." He sighs. "He really was amazing at tennis, though. Wasted potential."

"That's sad," I shake my head. The poor hot Ken-doll man is messed up in the head.

Mr. Walsh shakes his head in agreement. Then he holds his hand out to Heather. "I'll see you next week, once you've opened the accounts we've discussed. Then we can finalize paperwork."

Heather nods and guides me and my slumped shoulders outside.

We climb into her brand-new, cherry red Caddy. (Heather would not listen to anyone who told her this was a granny car. It was her granny's dream car and, by extension, hers. And now she has it.) So, we be ballin' like Nana Graham.

I stroke the leather seats and shove aside thoughts of the sexy Liar-Pants-On-Fire. I definitely don't want to see his pants burn to a crisp and reveal his muscular thighs and his—I shake my head to stop that thought. Nope. I refuse to let myself ogle a liar. Even just in my thoughts. In order to distract myself, I ask Heather, "So, how you gonna invest all this money?"

Heather shakes her head. "That was a whole lotta gobble-de-gook."

"Right?"

She sighs. "The car's fun. But that, that was—"

"Not fun," I supply.

She nods. "Way complicated. I've gotta set up like seven new bank accounts this week." She blows out a raspberry.

I smile. "How about Braum's burgers and ice cream? My treat."

We go through the drive thru and back to the little house I rent with two other women. Nobody's home, so Heather and I set up at the dining table and I prop my feet up on an empty chair as we eat juicy burgers.

"Winning the lottery should be exciting and fun and, like, carefree," Heather grumbles, pulling out a pickle and nibbling on it. "That asshat lawyer made me feel like an idiot for not having all this shit set up already. Like, dude, I just won."

I shrug as I take a final bite of my burger. "'Mo' money, mo' problems.'" Like I know or something.

She blows another raspberry. That seems to be a thing this afternoon. "What would you do with the money?"

I think about it as I stir my vanilla ice cream. "I dunno. Buy a house? But I'm not an adventurer. You are. What's like ... your ultimate fantasy?" I picture her on some yacht cruising around the world. Maybe even racing someone to make it more exciting. Heather loves to win.

Me? I just love peace and quiet when I'm not working. I'm around people all day at work. They buzz at you like hornets hopped up on meth. They want this and that and the other. By the end of the day, my ears just want silence. A house without roommates sounds awesome.

Heather eats her peach-jalapeno ice cream for a minute before she answers my question. I know the exact moment she figures it out, because she gets this shit-eating grin on her face.

"What?"

She bites her lip and widens her eyes at me suggestively.

Immediately, I retract my feet into my own seat. Whenever Heather starts to look like that, we're in for trouble.

"I have an idea. Of something I'd really like. But ... I'd need help. What if I hired you, Katie?" Heather shrugs nonchalantly.

Whenever Heather tries to be casual, it means she's about to try to talk me into strolling into crazytown with her.

"You already gave me a loan. I'm not taking any more of your damn money. If this is some trick to give me more—"

"It's not! I really need your help!"

I study her suspiciously, "Hire me for what, exactly?"

She stands, goes to my bookshelf, and grabs a book. She comes back and tosses it on the table. I quickly snatch it up.

"That is a signed copy of *The Lost and the Chosen*!" I scold.

She nods. "It's one of your dirty romance books, right?"

I arch a brow, "Not just any romance."

"It's the harem one, right?"

"You mean reverse harem?" They're my guilty pleasure.

One woman. Lots of men. Hot sweaty sex. What's not to love?

Heather nods toward the book and takes another bite of ice cream. She swallows and swings her spoon through the air. "I want that."

"What?" I'm lost, even though there's an intuitive pit in my stomach opening up. She's about to lead me down the rabbit hole. And my body's just prepping for the fall.

"I want a harem. Of dudes."

I watch her for a long minute, waiting for the punchline. She doesn't give me one.

"You're serious?"

"Yeah. I'm a millionaire now. Why the fuck not? Why settle for one guy? Have a couple and when one pisses me off, just bounce to the next for a couple days."

She says this as if that is emotionally possible. Of course, Heather's been ... different since her divorce. She's always been full of piss and vinegar, as my grandma liked to say. Her divorce only made that manifest tenfold. Me —on the other hand—I'm all sugar and spice. At least on the surface of things.

Heather's eyes narrow on me when I'm not immediately enthusiastic. "You love those books. Don't you want one, too? After you help me get mine, we can totally get you one."

I shake my head and bite my thick bottom lip. "Nope. I'm good, thanks." Today is the perfect example of why I can't handle guys. I was totally into the liar. Completely buying everything he said. I'm too gullible. Not to mention there's Jeremy. He's my secret fuck-buddy and I can't even handle him.

Think of the devil ... my phone buzzes with a text. It's Jeremy.

When are you free?

I tuck my phone onto my lap so Heather can't see. I text: *Can't tonight.*

I get a dick pic in response. I roll my eyes.

"Who's that?" Heather's leaning over the table. She grabs my phone before I can stop her. Her eyes widen. "You told me you ended things!"

I bite my lip guiltily. "Jeremy sucks as a boyfriend but ... *needs.*" I shrug weakly.

Heather narrows her eyes and texts Jeremy back. I don't even fight her. Then she says, "You don't need *him.* You need your own harem. We're totally doing this. I can hire your company and you can set up all kinds of crazy dates for me. OOOHHHH! I know. We can go to an island. Like one of those dating shows! And you can coordinate it! It will be amazing! Totally bomb."

My chest tightens with a combination of panic and excitement. "Umm..."

Heather starts rattling things off. "We can have group dinners, group dates, individual. Ooh, we can have like team-building exercises. And like secret challenges! OMG. It will be the best. You can help me make it the best, right?"

"Are you sure that's what—"

"Totally sure."

My mind starts to whirl with possibilities. Visions of what could be sparkle in my mind like little tiny diamonds. My eyes meet Heather's. She's so full of energy that if I touched her right now, I'm sure I'd get a shock. And all that energy is focused on me.

Can I pull this off? Could I organize something like this? It's gonna be big and wild and expensive. But it'll also be the most exciting thing I've ever done my whole life.

I bite my lip and give a slow nod. Heather jumps up, tosses my phone on the table, and starts jumping up and down. "I'm gonna get a harem! I'm gonna get a harem!" she chants in a sing-song voice.

I smile and shake my head as I pick up my phone, and as I expected, Heather's text to Jeremy says: *It's over.*

That text is true for pretty much every part of my old life. It's over. And if Heather has anything to say about it, my future is about to become an impossible cyclone of whirling, swirling crazy.

CHAPTER FOUR

Motherfucker! The people who run those dating shows do not have it easy, I think to myself as I get yet another quote for private islands. It looks like Heather's gonna have to shell out about eighty grand a night. Fuck. That thought makes me want to puke a little. That's almost three years of work at my old job.

Doc Stife has left messages. He doesn't really believe I'm quitting. But I'm so glad I am. I always meant to go out and do something else. But then the recession hit. And one thing that's a sure bet in Oklahoma is that people have let their mouths rot to hell. So, they end up needing the dentist.

Party planning? That was just a pipe dream. Just a fun little thing to daydream about while I stared at teeth with more holes than swiss cheese.

In the last forty-eight hours, that daydream has become a

reality. And it's awesome, terrifying, and overwhelming. I feel like I'm walking the tightrope over Niagra Falls like those crazy men did on TV before the internet took over. You only watched them waiting for a disaster to happen. I'm them. I'm trying to defy the odds and get this shit right on the first shot. I'm checking and double checking, and triple checking everything.

Heather wants a Bachelorette-style experience. She wants dresses and planned dates and excursions. She wants a bunch of hot guys to choose from. And I'm coordinating it all with four lists and over a thousand checklist items.

Whenever something gets boring—a lot of checklist items include ensuring we have belly medicine and passports—or the money side of things starts to make my stomach churn, I pull up a tab on my brand-new laptop and go back to searching for hot guys for the harem.

I have a dating service providing some, but I know what Heather likes—and more importantly, what the bitch actually needs—so I've been searching for younger doctors who'll be uptight enough to offset Heather's unique brand of psycho. She needs someone semi-rigid who'll indulge her but be busy enough to do their own thing.

I pat myself on the back when one guy named Andrew, a cutie with freckles who's working on being a surgeon, DMs me a 'yes.'

Score! I fist pump and stand up to dance around my living room. Heather walks in to find me shaking my ass in silence, celebrating my future brother-in-law, my future title as matchmaker of the century, and the basic brilliance that is me. I wave at her to join the silliness. When I notice her with her phone up, recording me, I freeze.

My hands lower in slow motion. "No, you didn't!"

"This is Insta-gold!"

I tackle her. "I just got a super-hottie signed up for your harem-quest, so you delete that shit right now or I'll take him back, missy!"

We play fight on the crappy green shag carpet until we find a cheeto that was somehow hidden in all the shag. It's so old the cheese is gone, and it looks like a deformed miniature finger.

"Gag! You're moving out of here, like now!" Heather sits up and pushes me off her. She holds up her phone and deletes the awful dance video. "Get your suitcase."

"Where the hell am I moving?" I ask. "Because it sure as hell won't be in with you."

We tried living together after high school. Both of us nearly murdered each other. Our love is best given with a bit of a distance. Or at least with breaks. Which is why I'm getting myself the farthest fucking condo from the chaos on this private island. I don't want to hear Heather's wild-monkey orgies with these guys.

And I'm pretty sure she's planning on orgies. She just added me to her online shopping account so I can use her card to order shit. The girl has ordered enough lube to grease the Holland Tunnel in New York City.

Heather clicks her tongue as she thinks. "I might just rent you an apartment near mine." She just moved into a swank apartment downtown, near the Blue Dome district, where all the bars and restaurants have that posh, pretend-we're-not-a-chain-restaurant-even-though-we-are feel to them.

"Um ... isn't it loud at night?" I ask. I'm totally a morning person. "What about something on Riverside?"

"Ugh, that's for retired people."

"Well, you're basically retired now—"

"Ew. Not even." She sweeps her hair back and I notice new purple peekaboos.

"Look, that's where I'd like to stay for now. I can pay for it, once you start paying me my salary."

She rolls her eyes. "Fine."

I spend the rest of the day moving the five bags of crap and the bed I own into an apartment that overlooks the Arkansas River. I realize I only own one chair. I set it up facing the balcony in my empty ass living room.

Heather was kind of bothered by that fact when she left.

I don't really care about furniture right now. I've got my own apartment. I'm a fucking party planner. And, in two weeks, I'm gonna be basking in the sun on a private island that comes with its own master chef, watching a gaggle of guys chase after Heather while she preens.

I sit in my lone chair, new laptop on my lap. I click 'reserve' on Thais Island in the Caribbean. As I do, I shake my head. Holy fuck. This is really happening.

Heather's won the lotto and I'm getting her a lotta men. Lott o' men, I correct myself, chuckling at my own pun. Heather's getting her own harem of lotto men.

THE NEXT TWO weeks are a shit-show of planning while we wait for Heather's money to come in. Who knew that so many guys would be cool with a harem relationship? But, like two hundred dudes volunteered on that dating service. So, I've had to scroll through making cuts. First round, I watched a lot of videos and read bios. I did that for like thirty guys and cut twenty-eight. But that took me nine hours. Nine! My neck was so sore after that I just starfished on the living room floor with a Salonpas slapped on my skin.

"I hate turning thirty," I moan as the doorbell rings with my Chinese delivery. I pull my lazy butt to the door and

Heather sweeps in past the Chinese delivery dude, all in a huff.

"You know what I just saw?" she asks.

I shake my head as I pay the delivery man.

"Shane Paul was just parading around his new girlfriend at Yokozuna."

"What's that?"

"The sushi place!" Heather makes this statement as if it should be obvious. Like I've eaten sushi before.

"I'm sure she's just as trashy as the others."

Heather's eyes flash and she swallows hard. I watch as she fights the tears. She and Shane Paul were high school sweethearts. Then he cheated. She forgave him. He cheated again. Since they've divorced, he's paraded around town with an endless line of bimbos.

"You wanna key his car?" That's been my go-to revenge tactic. Shane Paul's truck might be ten years old, but it's still his baby. And since the divorce, we've put probably sixty key scratches all over. When the break up was still fresh, we'd even let the air out of the tires.

Heather shakes her head. "I want to do something bigger. I have cash now. What the fuck can I do to him? What do rich people do to get back at each other?"

We spend a good half-hour eating Chinese and searching

the internet for revenge tactics. Ultimately, we decide on one. As the sun sets, we head over to the copy shop and pick up the newly designed posters someone on Fiverr made for us. We buy some staple guns and duct tape. Then we head over to Shane Paul's neighborhood. We staple the signs to every pole we can find. We duct tape them to fences. We giggle like drunk teenagers out toilet papering houses.

The signs say: "Missing: Precious Scrotum. If found, please return to Shane Paul Zurich." It has a picture of two hairy balls on it, which from far away, could be mistaken for someone's misshapen dog. It also has Shane Paul's phone number on it.

We finish posting the last of the signs and then climb into the Caddy. I lean back against the seat and sigh. "I wish we could hack Shane Paul's phone to listen to the messages he gets."

Heather smacks the steering wheel. "YASS! We're gonna do that."

I shake my head. "How?"

She shrugs. "I dunno. But I've got money now. So, we're gonna find a fucker and get it done."

It takes until two in the morning, but we do find a fucker. And get it done.

Heather's vicious look of victory is all the motivation I need to feel like we've done the right thing. Or at least, the morally-grey, subjectively right thing. His cheating and their divorce have ripped her up.

I hope to high heaven that this whole harem business can at least help her mend her heart. Fuck. I'm thinking like my grandmother. Well, I hope that at least Heather can get some screaming orgasms out of this and that she'll get over Shane Paul and that one-true-love crap she's held onto for too long.

The voicemail messages are solid gold. Every time I see Heather over the next week, she plays them for me.

"Have you looked under your totem for your scrotum?"

"Maybe you left your balls on the playground where you pick up those tramps you bring home. And stop speeding down the street!" Heather laughed when she played that one, saying it was their old neighbor Dane, who *hates* Shane Paul.

Another message came from an unknown caller. A breathy, phone-sex-worthy male voice said, "Excuse me. I was calling about the lost little scrotum. Is there a reward if I help you find *the precious*?"

One night, Heather shows me a text photo of some prunes someone left on Shane Paul's doorstep. She's pretty sure it was Dane again. A nice note accompanied the prunes. "Returned: Two balls. Slightly used. Reason for return: Did not meet expectations."

Some of my other favorites were quick jabs: "I just saw a squirrel eating your nuts."

"Look down past your fat gut!"

"Lost your balls? *Taint* nothin' you can do about it."

"Check your pool table. Or the golf range."

"Maybe your balls crawled up into your asshole when they saw your ugly face."

"Did you throw them out with the Christmas tree?"

"What the fuck you need balls for? Just get a woman to tell you what to do."

"You're responsible for putting away your own toys young man. It's your own fault if you lose them."

"Did you slap your scrotum around? Maybe it's got the balls to leave you."

Apparently, everybody loves a good ball joke. I'm pretty sure every neighbor called or did something to Shane Paul because of those signs. Even as I laugh at each and every ridiculous comment Heather shows me, it all just reinforces what I already know. People are jerks. Relationships aren't worth it. At the end of the day, my pain is just a punchline in someone else's joke. Laughed at one second, forgotten the next.

CHAPTER FIVE

The matchmaking company sent over another hundred pre-screened male candidates for Heather's harem. That's in addition to the two hundred I went through before. There's a box at my feet of rejected men and I still have seven folders left in my hands. I feel like I've stared at thousand photos of men. I don't know how fucking matchmakers do it. I could just let the company make the final picks, I guess. But something about that feels wrong. I stuck with it today, but now, I'm literally just flipping through the stacks and rejecting guys based on whether or not they have good teeth. I only read the file if their smile is good. I figure good teeth equals good hygiene and a dental plan, therefore a steady job. Or that's what I convince myself in order to justify my picks for the island. Heather only wants ten quality guys. She doesn't want to be too overwhelmed by choices. I picked out the new doc, an accountant named Tim, a personal trainer ... I forget the rest. I made sure the company didn't send over anyone in the oil and gas industry. Shane Paul's climbing that corporate ladder and all those big wigs know each other. I stare at the last seven files. I have one spot left. I sigh and pull a folder at random. Uno has a wild card right? Why not harems? Maybe fate will be at play and this guy will be the one.

I glance at his name. Jeremiah Bible. I snort. Yeah, chances of him being the one are slim to none. Once Heather hears that name, she's gonna run for the hills.

I toss him in the keeper pile anyway. There's still eight good choices and the new doc I'm holding out hope for in the mix. One rando shouldn't be a biggie. Who knows? Maybe he'll be some rock star. He had a leather jacket on.

I rub my eyes.

Heather bursts into my apartment. She's changed up her hair, going for a sleek, straight black with deep purple peekaboos.

"Nice hair," I tell her.

She waddles over to me and waves me out of my chair. She plops down, legs spread wide like a guy. "Brazil is the worst country in the entire world. How can women do this to themselves on the regular?"

I laugh. "You waxed?"

"It hurt like a bitch. Think I traumatized the poor Viet-namese lady who did it. Though you know what? She told me I needed hoo-ha surgery to tuck those lips back in."

My jaw drops. "She didn't!"

Heather nods, "I totally didn't tip her."

I shake my head and grab myself and Heather some sodas. "Good for you."

"I also might have told her I was gonna buy her shop and fire her 'cause she sucks at customer service. Can you help me do that?"

I burst into laughter. "Sure. Let me get right on that."

"I'll pay you more."

I roll my eyes. "You're already paying me too much." In addition to the loan, she's paying me for organizing this crazy-ass, harem-seeking island adventure.

Heather presses her lips together, "About that—"

"No! No more money!" I hold my hand up and take a sip of my soda. With the hundred fifty grand from this event, I'll be able to pay her loan back and put a down payment on a house. Maybe even upgrade my car to a newer one, if taxes work out. I'm currently driving a badass 1998 Acura with ripped seats that are hidden by seat covers. But it would be awesome not to get poked in the ass by ripped seat cushions while I drive. Or to have windshield wipers where the spray actually sprays and I don't have to carry around a water bottle with a hole cut in the lid so

I can squirt on glass cleaner any time I need to clean my windshield. I dream of a car built in the twenty-first century.

Heather snapping her fingers brings me out of my visions of semi-used Toyotas, slightly dented Dodge trucks, or grandma's prized Oldsmobile.

"Are you packed?" she asks.

I nod. "Yup."

A huge grin lights up her face. The mischievous kind. The kind she used to get when we were neighbors as little girls and used to sneak cookies at one house, only to go to the other and sneak more—our mothers none the wiser. "I can't believe this is actually happening," she says.

I grab my suitcase. "Me either. It's crazy."

I pick up the stack of winning candidate files and tuck them into my big-ass purse. "Ready when you are, H-bomb."

She rolls her eyes, "You'd better not tell anyone else that nickname."

"I won't." I smile. I won't unless she goes nuclear. Which is why the nickname is such a perfect fit.

She drives us to the airport, where we're supposed to meet a pilot for the private jet we hired. I'd never done it before. It's like Uber. Fancy-ass plane for hire by the hour. We fly out to this island, then it flies back, picks up the guys in Florida and brings them to the island. The pilot hangs out with us, on call for the excursions I've been frantically planning.

"So, this pilot's name is Alec Mars," I remind her.

"Ooh, a pilot, maybe I need one of those in the harem," Heather jokes.

We are led through the airport by a short guy in a black suit. He leads us around back to a hangar where a sleek, sexy white jet is waiting.

Staring at the jet makes everything feel more real. I've never been on a plane in my life. I've been to other towns in Oklahoma, but I've never left the state. Now, I'm headed to some tropical paradise. I stop and stare at the plane, letting reality sink into my skin like sunshine. A giggle bubbles out of my throat, and soon I'm laughing at the fact that this is my life. I mean it's Heather's lotto win, but everything in my life is about to change. Is changing. I can feel it. Once I step on that plane, I'm not just gonna be another small-town Okie girl who lives and dies on the streets her mama walked. I'm gonna have a stamp in my passport and a big-ass complicated event on my resume. I take a deep breath to calm myself.

A husky voice behind me asks, "First time on a private plane?"

"First time on any plane," I reply, turning to look at the speaker.

I have to look up, up, up. I'm 5'6" but the guy standing just behind me is massive. He's gotta be at least 6'3" and with his thick arms corded with muscles and his massive chest, I could easily imagine him playing football in high school or college. His black hair is shaved close to his head, his lips are only emphasized by the light scruff on his face, and his dark brown eyes ride the line between intense and very intense. They're like a smack on the ass. The good kind.

Right now, those eyes are focused on me. My cheeks heat.

"Sorry, I bet it's annoying to have a first-timer—"

His hand touches my shoulder, "Nope."

There's a moment where he stares, and I swear I see a hint of a smile on his lips. Just the slightest curl. That hint makes my knees tremble.

"I'm Alec. Your pilot." He pulls his hand away and he strides off, nodding to another guy in the hangar and stripping off his leather jacket.

I'm left shocked, dazed, mesmerized like a fucking cat with a laser light. I turn to watch him walk away. I can see his back muscles flexing under his collared shirt. Holy shit. I might need a fan. Or an AC. Or maybe a tiny igloo shoved onto my lady bits.

Alec the pilot is smoking hot.

Heather comes up beside me and appreciates the view as Alec checks something on the wings and then boards the

plane, his delicious ass muscles flexing beneath his
starched black pants. "He's not on my list of candidates,
so he's fair game," Heather says as she watches me visu-
ally assault Alec with my porn eyes.

My eyes snap over to her. "No. Don't even think it. Not
gonna happen. I'm working."

"Your panties just caught on fire in front of my eyes," she
says, way too loudly for an airport hangar. Her words
echo and Alec looks over.

"My face is the only thing catching fire right now," I hiss.
"Stop it."

"You deserve—"

"This trip is about you," I hold up a hand to stop her. "I
need to stay focused on you."

Heather chews her lip as she watches me, weighing how
serious I am.

"I'm serious," I tell her.

"I can see that. But, um, other things may already have
been set in motion."

My nostrils flare. "What did you do, Heather?"

She shrugs, innocently, picking at the fringe on her
brand-new designer purse. "I thought that maybe this trip
could be a learning experience for both of us."

I turn to look at her and narrow my eyes. "What's that supposed to mean?"

Heather holds up her hands. "I know you're upset about you-know-who. But you've carried that with you for years. And you've settled since. You knew Jeremy was a total dickwad and dated him anyway. And then took forever to break up. And then agreed to be fuck-buddies. Tell me the truth. Was that his idea?"

I shrug.

Heather shakes her head. "You're too non-confrontational. You just let people walk all over you."

"You included," I spit out.

She tilts her head and puts a fist on her waist. "Not the same thing. I'm not feeding you full of bullshit lies like your pussy isn't good enough or you aren't fun enough to be around, or—"

"You called me a stick in the mud five times last week."

"Only because you refused to get matching tattoos with me."

"I don't want your lotto number on my ass! It'll make me look like some kind of escaped prisoner."

Heather rolls her eyes. "Stick in the mud."

"See?" I wave a hand at her.

"Have you ever cried because of anything I've done?"

"I cried when you cut my doll's hair and gave her a mohawk."

"I was practicing for my future!" she gestures at her own hair.

"You could see all the pinholes. If you held her up through the light, it shone straight through her skull and dotted the sidewalk!"

"Now, you're just being dramatic."

"No, it happened."

"OMG. I'll buy you a new doll. Okay? We were kids. My point is, I don't make you cry. And you do stand up to me."

I raise a brow at her.

"You aren't getting a tattoo are you?" She takes my silence as affirmation she's right.

"Anyway, I was thinking ... you had, like, a really hard time being honest with Jeremy."

A black car pulls up outside the hangar and Heather's eyes flicker toward it before she settles her blue gaze back on mine. "I think you need to work on being honest. And calling people on their shit. So... I kinda hired someone to help with that."

I squint at her. "You hired me a fucking therapist? That's low. I'm not that fucked—"

"Not a therapist," she shakes her head and grabs my hand. She starts pulling me away from the plane and toward the black car.

"We don't have time for this," I grumble.

But that's when the car door opens. A man's tennis shoe pops out, followed by a lean, tanned leg, followed by sports shorts, a t-shirt, and a face that makes my jaw drop. I turn to stare at Heather, not believing what I'm seeing. She gives me a full-teeth sorry/not sorry smile.

"So, we meet again," a smooth tenor voice says.

I turn back to the guy who's slid out of the car. Danny, the liar from the law office, stands in front of me, his blue eyes twinkling.

I give Heather a what-the-fuck glare.

She gives me a little shrug and says, "I hired Danny to be our tennis and golf instructor. Did you know he plays golf, too?"

I don't respond. I'm fuming. I've had to coordinate endless events for this thing. Endless. I've sorted through half the damn males on the planet to find her some harem candidates. And she's saddling me with a fucking liar on staff? Why? To distract me? To torture me?

"Every time you call him on a lie, I'll pay you an extra five grand," Heather says. "But for every lie he gets away with, you lose five grand."

I explode. Inside, a huge anger bomb just bursts, shredding my guts and sending smoke out my ears. She's gonna fucking try and pull that kind of shit on me? "You can't do that!"

Heather shrugs. "Rich people are assholes. What can I say?" And with that, the rich bitch just walks away.

I glare up at the liar. "You'd better not make me lose any money."

He holds up his hands, pleading, "I'd never—"

I shake my head and start to walk away.

"She's paying me to be honest."

"That's a fucking lie," I shout back over my shoulder.

"Shit," he grumbles.

Suddenly, I'm hoping that I picked out ten crazy losers who will annoy the shit outta Heather. Because she's certainly just found a surefire way to annoy the shit outta me.

She's bribing me, threatening me, and torturing me all in one. My best friend shoulda' joined the army when that recruiter hit up our high school, insteada' just trying to get him to smoke pot with her by the track. She'd have made a damn fine general.

Fuck her.

This means war.

CHAPTER SIX

"Shot gun!" I call as I climb the steps and board the plane. I stride past Heather and make a hard left for the cockpit. I slide into a seat and pull out my laptop. I'm pissed.

Right now, I'm seriously considering changing one of Heather's dates from rock climbing to some donkey sex show. I google how to find those stupid-ass things and get sucked in by some video that claims boys fuck donkeys to make their dicks bigger. That's when a throat clears behind me.

"Umm..."

I turn to find Alec the hot pilot staring at my screen. As I stare up at Alec, a man on screen says, "I used to go into the hills every Sunday to fuck donkeys."

Shit! My entire body burns from embarrassment. I start to sweat. I can't believe he saw this. I can't believe I opened that tab. I was just so mad. I slam the laptop closed. "Sorry. Looking at revenge tactics."

Alec's eyes widen slightly, but his voice retains a dry steady tone as he says, "You're gonna force an ex to fuck a donkey?"

I sigh. "I wish. I was thinking of making you fly Heather to go watch a donkey sex show instead of taking her on one of the dates I planned for her group."

He nods, as if that's completely reasonable. "Well ... just let me know what you decide."

I let out a nervous laugh. "Will do. I take it you've had stranger assignments?"

He nods but doesn't explain. Then he gestures toward the plane's cabin. "It's time to take your seat."

I bite my lip and stare up at him. "I wanna ride shot gun, if that's okay."

He opens his mouth and I see he's about to make me go sit with the liar and the bitch so I rush to say, "Otherwise, I'm gonna do worse things to Heather than make her watch donkey sex."

Alec cocks his head. "She more than a boss to you?"

"Best friend. Since we were six."

Alec nods. "Alright then. But you have to move. That's my seat."

I go cherry red as I scramble to pack up my laptop and then try to scoot to the other captain's chair without rubbing my ass against Alec. I fail. Somehow. Even though I try to make myself as small as possible, when I shuffle sideways to the other seat, Alec's front rubs against my ass. I freeze. I'm not sure how to react. Fuck. His thighs are pure muscle. I can smell his cologne. It's soft, almost like baby powder mixed with spice. And I think I feel—

Alec moves into his seat before I can be sure. I sit in my new seat and just stew on my own embarrassment for a little while. I'm like a fucking cow chewing cud, just repeating that motion over and over again in my head. Did I really feel his thing? Did I?

But Alec doesn't say anything. So maybe he didn't think it was on purpose. Or at least, hopefully, he's not offended and doesn't think I did it on purpose. Hopefully, he's not mad at me and being quiet because he's mad at me.

I realize I'm letting my anxiety get away with shit. I try to shut it down and distract myself. I glance over my shoulder to check that Heather's seated in the cabin. As I do, I realize that there definitely should have been enough room for me to get past Alec without touching. He had plenty of room to move back in the aisle. My lady parts throb at that realization. Alec the hot pilot just rubbed against me. On purpose.

Like a stupid schoolgirl, this realization sends me

spiraling into shy mode. I can't look at him. Can't talk to him. Holy mother fuck. My palms get sweaty and I wipe them on my cheap sun dress. Suddenly, I'm embarrassed that I wore a cruddy blue flower print dress and cheap flip flops to fly on a jet. I wish I'd have let Heather buy me new clothes like she wanted. Expensive ones. Alec's probably used to seeing beautiful, well-kept rich women day in and day out. I'm probably just some strange, poor little weirdo to him. Double shitty shit fuck. I reach for my laptop again, but Alec's hand shoots out and wraps around my wrist.

Immediately, my thoughts go to visions of him pinning down both my hands as he—

"No electronics up here, sorry. It'll mess with my instruments."

I'll mess with your instruments, the naughty part of my mind says. But, of course, I do *not* say that out loud. Out loud, I just squeak, "Okay. Sorry. I didn't know." I give a nervous chuckle.

Alec stares hard at me for a moment, causing my nervous giggles to increase. Dammit.

He finally releases me and goes back to flipping dials and talking to someone through his headset.

I collapse back in my seat. My heart's beating like I ran a marathon. Damn. I haven't been this attracted to a guy since... since the liar. My eyes narrow as I hear Heather and Danny chatting happily behind me. I huff and grab a notebook out of my bag and start flipping through it, reviewing the zillion reservations I've made. I cross and uncross my legs, deciding airport jet seats aren't all that comfortable. At least not in the cockpit.

When Alec's voice comes over the loudspeaker, I nearly jump out of my seat.

He announces that we're cleared for takeoff to Thais Island.

I start to buckle up.

"You don't have to do that, you know," Alec glances over at me before swiping at some buttons on his touchscreen.

"What?" I ask as I pull my belt tight.

"Those things just provide the illusion of safety. If we fall from the sky at 800 miles per hour—"

A zillion screaming visuals assault my mind. All of them involve horrid fiery crashes that end up with us smacking into the ocean at full speed. I hold up a hand. "I like my illusion of safety, thanks."

Alec nods and gets back to work.

I sit there, trying to avoid thinking about all the ways we could crash. I try to distract myself and think of the last movie I saw Chris Hemsworth in. Then the last movie I saw him shirtless. That works. I shake my head as the fear clears up. Why did he have to say that? "I think you may have ruined flying for me," I scold.

"I was hoping you'd get pissed enough at me to go sit back with your friend, actually," Alec confesses.

My heart falls. "I'm sorry, am I bothering you?"

His eyes flicker over to me, but he doesn't make eye contact. His eyes dance across my legs before he looks back at his instruments. "More like ... distracting." He swallows and I watch his throat contract.

There's something adorably nervous about that. This big brute of a man being distracted by me. I lean forward as we pull out of the hangar and onto the runway. "You're kicking me out of your cockpit?" I smack my hands over my mouth when I realize how dirty that sounds.

Alec gives me a full-blown smile as he pulls back the controls and we taxi down the runway.

I get caught up in his smile for a second before I realize—shit. We're about to take off. My heartrate spikes. My hands clamp down on the armrests. I close my eyes take a deep breath and blow it out slowly through my lips.

Next to me Alec growls.

My eyes pop open and I glance over, concerned. Is something wrong? Are we about to crash? Nope. His hands aren't on the controls—WTF!? He's adjusting himself. There!

He catches me looking and groans again.

"Yup. You are kicked out."

My jaw drops. "Seriously?" It's not my fault he ... oh, maybe it is. But I didn't do anything on purpose. "Look, I can't go back there. I won't talk. Okay?"

I yank down my skirt, but the motion draws his eyes to my chest and he just clutches the joystick in his right hand harder. "Go. Now."

Ass! I didn't even do anything. But, if I'm distracting him, fine. I'll go. I don't want the stupid plane to crash. I'll go and sit with the sharks. I look back and I see Heather eyeing me gleefully. I glare at her as I unbuckle my seat.

"Fine. Send me away. But you saw how I plan revenge on those who piss me off." I grab my bag and shuffle into the aisle.

I start to walk away, and I hear Alec mutter, "Revenge sex."

I whirl around to watch him. "What?" My heart pitter patters in my chest. Nervously. Did Alec just say he wanted revenge sex? My entire body clenches at the thought of clutching his bulging biceps.

Alec doesn't look back at me as we gain speed down the runway. "Revenge sucks. You should give it up."

I'm strangely disappointed that the hot guy I just met didn't actually proposition me for revenge sex. Dammit brain. Get out of the gutter. I stick out my tongue at Alec. But only because he can't see it.

I walk down the aisle and plonk down as far from

Heather's smug face and Danny's curious one as I can get. Now I'm pissed at her for breaking up with Jeremy, too.

I haven't had sex in weeks and now I'm having horny ass thoughts about a stranger.

Danny stretches and his abs peek out under his shirt. Two strangers! Ugh. I wish just once I could get back at her!

But Alec's right. Revenge sucks. It sucks because I don't actually have the guts to get it.

CHAPTER SEVEN

I fall asleep. I never knew plane rides could be so lulling. But there's something about the way we just coast through the air that's so much more soothing than driving. Maybe because I'm used to driving in Oklahoma, which is an experience that alternates between rattling around on dirt roads and inadvertently clicking my teeth together as I drive on paved roads with potholes the size of a Great Dane. About halfway through the flight, I jolt awake to find a line of drool sliding down my cheek and a jacket tossed over my shoulders. It's not my jacket. It's a crumpled, blue, man's jacket. I sit up.

Danny the liar sits across from me, eating chips and smirking as I wipe my face and glare at him.

"You look cute when you sleep."

I roll my eyes. "Yeah, right."

"I think we got off on the wrong foot."

I yawn and stretch my sore neck. I'm too tired to play games right now. Wrong foot is a total understatement. I pull down the jacket when my mind wakes up enough to realize it's his. I hand it back and say, "Oh?"

Our fingers touch as he takes the jacket from me. And I completely quash whatever sensation that creates. Because the pilot is now better qualified for my nighttime finger fantasies than this Liar-Liar. Even if I've always had a bit of a soft spot for blonds.

I rub my eyes and try to avoid looking at Danny's light blue eyes as he stares at me.

"Since we're going to be working together, I thought it'd be good to bury the hatchet."

I nod. "Consider it buried." In your back. "I've got to go over some things before we land."

"I could help. I once worked at a—"

"Are you about to lie?" I ask.

Danny's head jerks back like I've smacked him. His blue eyes widen with hurt and lock onto mine. "Of course not. I think you must be paranoid because of what Ben said. Look, my brother wasn't telling the truth. He has a bit of a condition, we don't like to talk about it, but he got in this car accident a few years back. Head on collision when he was driving home late from a deposition." He rubs his hands together and shakes his head sadly.

Despite myself, I feel a twinge of sympathy.

Danny continues, "He moved in with me because he needed help. He couldn't walk for a while or anything. I drove him to physical therapy, helped him at home. Anyway, physically, he's recovered, but sometimes he just kind of gets confused..."

OMG. I was just totally getting sucked into his story. Danny is a damn good storyteller. Fuck. My eyes widen. I cover my mouth and tilt my head as Danny prattles on. He's as good as a damned TV actor, eyes tearing up when he talks about how proud he was when he helped his brother walk again.

Is he serious? I feel myself waver. This has to be a lie, right? His brother owns a law firm. He couldn't do that and be unhinged the way Danny's describing. I laugh nervously as I watch him. This has to be a joke, right? He and Heather and pranking me, testing me ... but he's still talking. Describing his brother's rough road to recovery, alcoholism ... Ok, time to call him out. Time to tell him he's full of it. I hope Danny's not someone who reacts badly. I mean, his brother called him out before. But the guy could probably take him. I mean, he didn't have the same muscles—Danny's muscles are on display in his casual sports attire, cut calf muscles, thick forearms, bulging biceps—but his brother was able to tell him off without Danny turning into a fist-wielding crazy. Hopefully I can, too. But I don't want to make him too mad. I just have to say it gently. Nicely. I take a deep breath—

"Five grand down," Heather calls out from her seat across the aisle.

I glare over at her and her unruffled hair and her non-drooly, now rich-girl face. What a bitch! "I was about to tell him."

"You were not. You did your nervous laugh. You were about to say, 'Oh, really? I didn't think your brother was that bad.' Or some other bullshit."

"Was not!"

"Yeah you were."

"You can't just take away five grand because I didn't call him out fast enough."

Heather holds a hand to her ear, "What's that? Did you want to go down ten?"

I see red. I clench my fists. "This is why I said I didn't want your money. Mixing money and friendship is a bad idea."

"I agree," Danny shrugs. "Mixing family and money is a bad idea, too. You have no idea what a monster my brother is. He's borrowed so much cash—"

"Lie." The word is out of my mouth before I process.

"Nope. Not a lie," Danny says. But his face droops a bit. "I really don't try to lie all the time. And it's only ever about little things."

My eyes widen. I swallow. But no frickin' way I'm letting Heather dock another five grand from my pay. I sigh and force the words out of my mouth. "That's a lie. You just said your brother got in a car wreck. That's not a little lie."

Danny shakes his head. "He did! That wasn't a lie."

I turn to glare at Heather. "He says he told the truth. How the hell do you know?"

"I text Ben and ask," she shrugs, pointing at the cell phone in her lap. Then she takes a sip of a mimosa that she somehow got from somewhere.

I want a mimosa. And some Tylenol. I'm gonna need it, dealing with these two. I tilt my head and stare at Heather. "Since I'm running this shindig for you, I'm technically his boss, right?" I'll just order the fucker not to talk to me. If he can't talk, he can't lie. Can't lie, then I can't lose five G.

Heather gives me an evil grin. "Nope. He reports directly to me."

My eyes narrow as my anger shifts from Danny to her. "Excuse me." I grab my computer bag and march up to the cockpit. I throw myself down in the co-pilot's seat.

"What—"

"Deal with it," I snap. "I cannot be back there right now."

Alec turns back to his instruments. "They deserve worse than donkey sex revenge?"

"Way way worse."

"Might I suggest the mating of ostracods? They vomit to attract the opposite sex."

A huge, earsplitting grin crosses my face.

"That sounds awesome."

Alec takes a second to turn his gorgeous head and smile at me. "I'll set it up. But, one condition. You have to come. So, we can watch them together."

My "hell yes" is only the tiniest bit breathy. Fucking shit. Is it too fast to fall for a guy in a couple hours? I mean, hotness and revenge in a single package? What more could a woman want?

Honesty, the wounded part of my heart shouts from the tiny little box where I've locked it up. You want honesty. And loyalty—

I shove that bitch back in her box and smile at Alec.

I only need those if things get serious.

And that is never gonna happen.

CHAPTER EIGHT

Alec drops us off at the island midday. It is glorious. White sand, water so clear you can see the seashells in the sand three feet below the surface of the waves, hills with gorgeous tropical foliage (that I'm pretty certain has all been imported). But, the ambiance ... I feel like I've just stepped onto a movie set. Like there's no way this could be real life. I've grown up with hills, lakes, trees and green galore, but it does not compare. There's salt in the breeze and everything just smells cleaner, better, magical. If that's a thing. I take a photo with my phone and text it to Olivia. She texts back: *I hate you.*

I send a smiley.

She texts me: *Also, some weird big ass looking dudes came by mom and dad's asking about Heather.*

I roll my eyes. *Probably more fake family members trying to get cash.*

Don't worry. Mom shot them down. She said they were scary looking.

I laugh and text her back: *I can't imagine anything scarier than mom.*

Right? Ok. At work. Have fun.

I let the water lap at my feet for a moment and just soak it all in. I don't have long to savor the moment though. I help Heather get set up in the master villa and then I get to work.

I spend the next four hours running around like a frizzy-haired monster setting up events, running through the forest to check on all the 'special activities' the staff prepped per my instructions, and checking to make sure each villa is clean, has towels, has fresh flowers — I don't trust the local staff. This is my event, and if something goes wrong it's on me. Every room has a plate full of hard candies on the bar table and I end up sneaking some from each room. The pineapple are okay, the blueberry need work. The orange-flavored ones are my favorite. They're a bright burst of flavor. I suck on them and hum as I straighten tablecloths and plump couch cushions. My annoyance at Heather, and her decision to bring Danny along, fades as I work.

Heather's always liked to push my buttons when she thinks it will cause me to 'grow.' Of course, she and I have very different ideas about healthy growth. She once invited me to a threesome with her and her husband. Her attempt to expand my horizons was my idea of icky weirdness. I did not wanna see Shane Paul's ding-a-ling no matter how many times I'd heard it described. Nope. Hard pass.

After I'm done with the villas, I go to the big banquet hall in the main villa. The bouquets are breathtaking, and the cutlery is the fanciest I've ever seen. I think it might even be silver. I study a fork. It hits me that this is real. I've only ever used plastic forks in every wedding I've planned. Even on the biggest day of their life, no one in my family could spring for more than barbecue. I trace the side of the fork.

"I hope you're not about to start combing your hair with that and singing."

I take my eyes off the fork and realize that there's a man standing in front of me. The chef's assistant, I guess. He looks like he's in his mid-thirties. He's not too tall. Maybe 5'9". He's got an impish, guy-next-door look with brown eyes and brown hair, thick scruff and a smile that takes him from normal to handsome.

"The Little Mermaid couldn't sing," I correct him as I put down the fork. "She'd lost her voice. You need to brush up on your Disney."

He chuckles and I immediately fall in love with the sound. Some people just have a laugh that's infectious. This guy is one of those. You can tell, when he's happy, he makes everyone around him happy.

I hold out a hand, "I'm Katie McPherson."

"Kenneth Wilson. Are you one of the new guests?"

"I'm the event planner for this crazy shindig. Katie."

He shakes my hand with a grin. His hands are scarred and calloused, but for some reason the texture isn't off-putting. I have to stop myself from turning over his hand and looking at each little scar. He doesn't call me on my lingering handshake as I clear my throat and drop his hand.

Instead, he smiles and asks, "Shindig?"

"I'm from Oklahoma. Probably gonna end up using a lotta weird words. Just go with it. I was hoping to talk menus with the chef. He hasn't answered my calls or emails." We'd booked last minute, sliding into a cancellation after some CEO got fired or something and had to cancel his vacation. I'd cry for him, except I'm pretty sure he's gliding around on his golden parachute somewhere. "I've been trying to reach the chef to nail down the menu details, but haven't been able to get through," I tell Kenneth.

I'd only been able to send emails to the generic staff email, and the kitchen phone had always gone to voice-mail I fucking hope the chef was able to get the ingredients for drunken turtle pie for tonight. That's Heather's favorite dessert.

"Oh, well, our event manager got called away last week. I

think he might have known the man who passed away whose spot you took."

Kick me in the head. I'm an asshole. I'm so glad I didn't say anything I just thought about CEOs aloud. I try not to let the alarm show on my face. I put on a fake grin instead.

Kenneth shakes his head. "But even if we had gotten your emails or calls ... the head chef here is a little bit of an prima donna."

"What?"

"He doesn't do dictation. He creates what feels right for the moment."

I swallow hard. I blink several times, trying to tamp down on my annoyance. I smile brighter to hide it. "That ... wasn't something the booking agent told me."

Kenneth bites his lip and shrugs apologetically. "I don't know what to say. The chef's a dick."

I take a deep breath and stare up at the ceiling. The chandeliers look like something out of a fairytale. At least there's that. But I'd spent like twenty hours on menus, trying to think up shit that would fill guys up and ride the line between fancy and down-home goodness. I'd looked up recipes. Researched. And I hate cooking—even just reading about cooking. I'd fucking googled what the hell ghee was. Because I don't use 'clarified butter' at home, dammit. Who the fuck does?

I lick my lips and press them together. I'm letting myself get too worked up. And it's not like it's Kenneth's fault his boss is some five-star weirdo. Of course, the chef here would be. I should have expected it. He works here on a private island for millionaires who probably bitch like babies over every little thing. Who'd walk all over him if he let them. The chef's not an asshole. He's just trying not to have twenty-eight special dishes to prep each night for snobby assholes who only eat fruit if it's fresh from the orchard. This isn't a personal attack. This chef doesn't hate me. He doesn't know me. This is just how it is. Welcome to dealing with those who deal with richness.

I swallow my disappointment. "Okay. Okay," I look back at Kenneth, who's silently eyeing my mini-meltdown. Great. I smile weakly. "Can I just see the menu your boss came up with?"

Kenneth's grin grows wide. He winks. "He generally likes to keep it a surprise, but ..." he glances around conspiratorially to ensure we're alone and then leans in, "Maybe just this once." His hand comes up and he pushes back a strand of my hair.

When he's touching me, Kenneth's guy-next-door aura takes a turn. His eyes dilate and he keeps them locked on me as he leans in further and tucks that strand of hair behind my ear. His face is only inches from mine, and I can see the flecks of amber in his eyes. I smell cumin and fresh bread on him, and a wild mix of other scents that assault my nose with a rainbow of smells.

I can't help how my body responds to his nearness. My breathing instantly speeds up. Blood rushes to my cheeks. Fuck. Maybe it's the tropical air. I've never been this horny before. I've never been turned on by three guys so quickly.

Is it because I don't have Jeremy to scratch that itch anymore? Is it the dirty thirties? I've heard of that ... Or is there something in the water in Oklahoma that makes the guys there less attractive? Like some kind of chemical that puts a damper on their testosterone. Maybe Danny and Alec and now Kenneth have been like a one-two-three punch. Maybe after all these years, that good-guy-next-door vibe is my downfall. I've been avoiding guys like that for years. Guys who seem good-hearted. Guys who seem like they could envision something long-term. Nope. I've avoided them in favor of the Jeremy's of the world. Quickies and disappointments. Those are my jam.

Until now. I stand, frozen, but enraptured, as Kenneth leans in and his lips come close to my right ear. He stays there for a moment, a warm trail of air blowing up and down my ear, then along my neck. Shit. I have to fight against arching my back and shoving my neck onto his lips.

"Um, did you say something?" I ask, throat tight.

"Not yet."

I laugh uncomfortably. "Oh, I thought I didn't hear you."

I take a step back. I can't stand the tension. It's gonna make me do something completely unprofessional.

Kenneth's eyes twinkle playfully. He doesn't explain his hovering.

I give a big, fake grin and say, "Is creepy breathing the normal way to greet people here?"

"You smell like our handmade orange candies." He wags a scolding finger at me.

Relief floods me. Oh. That's what it was. He smelled the candy. I toss up my hands. "Busted. Shh. Don't tell anyone. There might not be any left in any of the rooms."

His brows raise. "You stole them all?"

"I prefer sample. I sampled them. The orange just happened to be the best."

"Better than the pineapple?"

"That was too creamy," I wrinkle my nose.

He gets thoughtful for a moment. "I always thought of the pineapple like soft afternoon sunshine, whereas oranges are that bright midday sun that just punches you in the face with flavor."

I smile at his poetics. "Guess I've never thought of food in detail like that before."

"Try it. What's pineapple taste like to you? If pineapple was an emotion, how would that feel?"

If pineapple was an emotion? Maybe this guy's drank one too many Mai Tais. But I can't say that to him. I worked food service in high school. The fastest way to get your steak dropped on the floor before it's served to you is to start some beef with the chef. Or his assistants. "Ummm. I think of pineapple as more flirty and fun. But those candies were all like pineapplely milk. Milk is not flirty. Milk is blah."

He taps his lip. "Hmmm… interesting. What about the blueberry?"

I shrug and wave my hands in a so-so gesture. But something in his face makes me halt, mid-gesture. "Oh, wait. You didn't make those did you? Cause it was all good. Just … I happened to like orange best."

Kenneth smiles. "Tell me more about the blueberry. Too bland like pineapple? Or what?"

I swallow hard. He totally did make them! Crap. I just insulted his work.

"I need to know what you thought. Details. Like the pineapple." He takes a step closer.

My heart rate ratchets up. Fuck. I don't want to tell him. But he grabs my hand and blinks down at me, batting his lashes. And I'm suddenly very aware of how fucking adorable he is. "It's important," he whispers. His thumb traces the inside of my wrist.

It's like my wrist has an on-switch wired to my mouth.

The truth just spills out automatically. "Blueberries aren't really sweet. They're like, I dunno, the goth berry. They don't taste like happiness."

His smile is blinding. "Brilliant."

I smile back, relieved and maybe … something else. Something I can't quite identify.

But then Kenneth's pretty brown eyes narrow and his mood changes on a dime. "Wait. Why were you in *all* the rooms? You don't trust our staff?"

"No!" I lie, stepping back and holding out a hand to wave off any offense. "No, that's not it. This is my first huge event like this. And so, I'm just paranoid. Plus, Heather's my best friend and I don't want to disappoint her. I just wanted to make sure everything was good before her guys arrive."

He nods. "Ah. First time. Got it. First time I had to make a five-course meal to pass a class, I had to have a trash can next to me. Puked three times. But I got through it. Because I wanted to graduate and get to call myself a chef."

I nod like a bobble head. Because he gets it. That's how I feel. This isn't school and there's no pretty diploma or title for me at the end. But paying off my loan, putting this on my website, and hitting Mom with an 'I told you so' seem just about as real and important as any piece of paper with a gold sticker and a white-haired man's signature. I wave my hand and say, "Yes. Like that. But, without the puking. Hopefully."

I start to smile when it hits me. I'm such an idiot. I go white as I stare at Danny. "*You're* the chef."

He raises an eyebrow. "What gave me away?"

"You said you're a frickin' chef."

He shrugs. "I like to make my own menus. So sue me."

I rub my eyes. I already have Danny playing games with me. I don't have the energy or the patience for someone else.

I turn away from Kenneth. I don't even know how I'm going to handle him. All I know is I'm not going to right now. I check my watch and pray evening's getting close enough that I can leave without any more awkwardness.

Score! For once, my watch is in line with my wishes. The guys will be here in about half an hour. I hope Heather's getting ready. My heart starts to pound, and I press my lips together. I try to remind myself that I get this adrenaline rush before every wedding. Only this is not a simple outdoor wedding. It's far from it. It's Heather's tropical orgy dream. "It's almost time."

"You mad at me?" Kenneth asks.

I half turn and give him a fake smile over my shoulder. "I just wish you'd told me. Now, I feel like an idiot."

He waves that off. "Don't."

I start walking off, but he calls out behind me. "Quick question. I heard this incoming group is a sex cult?"

I let out a harsh, booming laugh. I can't help turning around, because I have to see the look on his face. Is that ... hopeful? I squint and study his face. I don't know him well enough to be sure the expression was hopeful. But maybe. I say, "Not quite. Or not yet anyway. I wouldn't put it past Heather to start a religion outta it."

"But ... the things that have been scheduled ..."

I shake my head. "I really wish *someone* had read my emails all the way through." He either doesn't get it or else he ignores my passive-aggressive jab. "Heather wants to create a male harem. This is the culling. The trials, the ..." I search for another metaphor because Kenneth still looks confused.

He furrows his brow. "I'm sorry, a male what?"

My face heats. I can't believe I have to explain this to a staff member. At least it's not my mother, I tell myself. I clench my hands uncomfortably. Why am I having trouble talking about this?

He's just a stranger. Just a chef. Poor guy is probably gonna end up seeing way more than he ever wanted to in the male genetalia department. I should be able to just give him a quick rundown, right? But, my stupid tongue ties itself into a knot and refuses to come undone.

I reach into my bag and pull out a copy of *Sunshine and*

Bullets, a hot-as-fuck dark read that I've been using to get myself through the Jeremy-free days. It's easier than explaining to him. Particularly when I'm kind of annoyed at him right now. "Here. Read this. It'll help you understand."

He takes it from me suspiciously.

"Not a reader?" I ask. "That's cool. Just skip to page 197." There's a delicious scene there where one of her guys admits how much he liked watching. How cool he is with sharing after that. "I gotta go check on Heather." I take a deep, centering breath.

Kenneth puts his hand on mine. "It'll all be okay."

I nod. My thoughts are already flying to Heather. I need to check that she's dressed. It's a formal dinner tonight. And for Heather, that will mean a three-hour hairdo. If she hasn't already finished her hair, we're gonna be in trouble. I have ten hungry men who're about to land. I don't want this trip to turn into a *Lord of the Flies* situation. I look down and realize that Kenneth's still holding my hand. Also, my hand is shaking slightly. I meet his eyes. Words escape me. What comes out is: "Heather. Food. Book—don't bend the pages." At least I stutter out the important things.

Kenneth nods. "It'll all be fine. Dinner will be amazing."

I head out the door quickly. I double my speed when I take a quick look back and realize that Kenneth is just watching me walk away. After I round the corner, I swipe at my skirt, hoping that he wasn't staring at how wrinkled it was. Nope. He wasn't. My fingers close on a crinkled square of cellophane. I yank it off only to find part of a pineapple candy stuck to it. Great. Half-eaten candy has been stuck to my ass. What a way to make a great first impression.

Normally, I would stress over embarrassing shit like that. But, tonight, I don't get a chance. Because Danny, the lying tennis instructor, trots over to me and says,

"You told a lie."

"What? No, I didn't," I scoff.

"You did check all the rooms because you don't trust the staff. I watched you crawl around on the floor in my room and check for dust bunnies under the bed."

My face turns fuchsia. "How do you know that?"

"I was there," he says smugly. "I'd just hopped out of the shower."

I whirl around. I'm pissed after this afternoon, after Kenneth's stupid deception made me look the fool, and now Danny's trying to call *me* out? "No, you weren't! I checked in the bathroom!"

"Not in my room. You must be confusing my room with someone else's."

"I checked every room!"

"I'm asking Heather if I can get extra cash every time you lie," Danny gives me a smug face.

I clench my fingers so I don't smack him. "I'm not the one with a lying problem."

"Yes, you are."

"No, I'm not."

"Oh, then it's worse. You're delusional," he taunts.

I growl and stomp all the way to Heather's villa. I throw her door wide open and shout into her living room, "Heather! I'm pretty sure I can commit murder here and not get tried for it."

She comes around the corner, her hair still in curlers. When she sees Danny standing beside me, she grins. "She got pissed enough to threaten you with death?"

He nods.

She narrows her eyes. "Threaten you to your face?"

He shakes his head.

I balk. "What the mother fuck? You'll tell her the truth?"

Heather grins. "Danny, you just earned yourself a raise. Keep up the good work."

I yank at my hair as I stomp off into the night. If she wasn't my boss right now... If I hadn't quit my job... If I wasn't stuck on a deserted island... who the fuck am I kidding? Whatever

I do to Heather, she'll have no problem coming back at me twice as hard. I need to be zen. I need to be a zen duck. Let it roll like water off my back. A zen rubber duck. Whatever they do needs to bounce off of me and stick to them…

I need to stick it to them.

I'm so ready for Alec to land. Because I need to ruin another of Heather's dates.

CHAPTER NINE

Aline of dudes stumbling off a plane does not look like it does in the TV shows. There are no GQ winks and hands in the pockets, no confident descents down the stairs that are built into the swing-down jet door. There's yawning, stretching, bed hair (the non-sexy kind), wrinkled shirts, and a stale smell wafts from the plane that might be farts mixed with gym socks. In the dim light of an April evening, I can hardly match these guys to their hot pictures.

Fuck. These assholes better clean up good or Heather's gonna yell at me.

I've cleaned up decently, at least for me. And in under ten minutes, too. My hair's up in a no-nonsense bun, I'm wearing a pastel blue suit that's got a slightly risqué slit up the right thigh, and super cute flower-patterned heels —an outfit Heather surprised me with but makes me feel totally and one-hundred percent professional planner.

The only thing that would make it more official was if I had a headset with a microphone. And maybe one of those clipboards.

The men line up in front of me and I do a quick head count before I start making announcements. Eight, nine, ten, eleven... eleven?! I double check, thinking maybe Alec came down and I counted him in ... but I definitely would have noticed if Alec came down.

Nope, a quick scan shows me Alec is not lined up in front of me. Instead, I do a double take. Two guys, in matching shirts, with matching grins, matching eyes, and huge matching biceps grin down at me. Twins.

I didn't fucking pick any twins! I mean, the face looks familiar. So, maybe I picked one of them. I'm not sure and my fingers itch to double check my files. I mentally kick myself for not thinking about it in the first place, because it's total harem gold, but I eye the two suspiciously. How did both get on the plane? We had a roster. I know one of my picks got sick and replaced at the last second by the matchmaking company. But they didn't tell me they sent two guys. I didn't really open that file on the flight like I should have, though. I'll ask the twins to walk with me and see what's up. I've been busy with way more than just checking the rooms and the menus since we landed—the activities Heather wants are fast and furious —so I haven't checked my phone. Maybe the match-making company sent one extra as, like, a bonus? They should, considering the amount of money Heather dropped.

I shake my curiosity off so I can deal with the matter at hand. Introductions.

I put on my hostess smile and spread my hands wide. Then I feel stupid and clasp my hands together as I give the speech I practiced forty times in the mirror. "Welcome to Thais Island. We're so excited to have you here to meet with Heather Graham. Over the next three weeks, you'll get to know her and see if you are compatible with her and one another. Be ready for a wild ride, guys. I know you all have agreed to be open to an unconventional relationship and let me tell you, the path to getting there with Heather is also going to be ... unconventional. There are going to be lots of adventures ahead for you. The first week or so will focus on group dates to test your compatibility. Then there will be some competitive games to showcase your *skills*." I give my practiced wink and then continue, "I'm hopeful that tonight is the start of a wonderful future for several of you and Heather. As a reminder, right now, she's looking to settle into a relationship with three men. Just to be clear, if—at any time—you or Heather decide you aren't compatible, I will escort you back to this very plane and your time here will come to a close."

Alec appears in the doorway of the plane. He doesn't descend the steps, just leans against the open doorway and smirks down at me. His attention immediately makes an electric buzz run under my skin, which makes me stumble over my words and feel as clumsy as a newborn calf. My cheeks burn as I wrap up, "I'm Katie McPherson. I'm the event coordinator, so if you have any questions or need anything, please, don't hesitate to ask."

My speech is met with a few nods, some blinking, and one sneeze. Overall, not the glorious fireworks and cheering kind of response I'd hoped for. But I write it off as jetlag. Besides, I don't have time for cheers. I've got men to get to their rooms, a dinner to oversee, and the first interview to pull off...

I hand out maps that I printed at home on my new handy-dandy laser printer. "Here are your villa assignments. You each have a private room with an en-suite bathroom. Two men to each two-bedroom villa."

One guy grabs his phone and asks me, "Can I take a quick pic with you? This is just so awesome!" When a guy who looks like he belongs on a firefighter calendar asks me to take a picture with him, I have a rule: don't say no. In fact, that rule applies to anything that guys as hot as firefighters ask. I smile and lean in close, placing my hand on his rock solid chest as he snaps a picture of us. He turns around and snags one of the jet.

"What's your name?" I ask.

"Anthony Drake." He puts out a hand and we shake. He's the only blond in Heather's group since she tends to prefer the tall, dark, and handsome type. But he's got a great smile.

I turn back to the group and say, "I'll lead you all toward your villas right now, so you can freshen up before dinner. Each of you should find a tux in your closet. Tonight's dinner will be a formal event. The staff will bring your bags down in the next few minutes."

I turn back to the stairs to look up at Alec, but he's already disappeared back into the plane. Dammit. I'll have to hunt him down later to talk revenge tactics.

The men and I start down a path lined with palm trees and bird of paradise flowers.

I walk over to the twins as the men march off toward the gorgeous, uber-modern white villas that dot the island and surround a central pool.

"Hi, there," I extend my hand to shake the twins'. The huge, hulking men stop to shake and it's like arm wrestling with bears. They are that big and ripped, both slightly tan, with downturned hazel eyes and big pouty lips. I swallow hard. They're super-hot. Like, not my type hot—I'm totally intimidated and appreciative, but there's no chemistry (unlike the vinegar and baking soda volcano Kenneth or Alec or even Danny make in my stomach)—but the twins could definitely put those muscles to use modeling underwear or something. "I'm so sorry but I don't remember selecting twins and I selected each of the men to come down here."

The twins exchange a look and then smile back at me.

Twin One speaks, his voice deep and edged with the slightest Russian accent, "I'm Rubin and this is my brother Reval. And we do everything together."

"Everything? I'm pretty sure that ..."

Rubin winks.

I press my lips together. I'm pretty fucking sure that if I send one of these guys home Heather will have a fit. I haven't heard that twin sex is on her bucket list, but I'm sure once she sees these two, it's gonna get added. But an extra guy? That's gonna throw a wrench in all my plans. "I don't have any more rooms."

"We can share. We love sharing. *Everything*."

I gloss over the innuendo there because I have more important things to think about. Like goddamned tuxes and the special revenge-on-Heather slideshow for tonight and—I take a deep calming breath. Thank goodness I'm a planner.

Heather and I were in Girl Scouts one year and our group mom was a super over-planner. "Two is one and one is none." Thank frickin' goodness I worshiped that woman and her ability to help us make tissue paper and pipe cleaner flowers. Because that motto is now gonna let Heather consider whether or not she wants to cream in the middle of a twin sandwich. I chuckle at my own naughty pun and the twins look at me curiously.

"You both are lucky that I ordered some extra tuxes in

case something was wrong with one. Follow me." I lead the twins toward my villa, which is currently less of a gorgeous home and more of a warehouse, as full as I had the staff pack it with boxes of supplies. I weave through the box-maze and grab an extra tux from the hall closet. Then I tell the twins, "Now, I'm making an exception for you guys, here, so prove me right."

"Yes, ma'am." They hurry off to their cabin.

I go to check that Heather's slipped into the Moulin Rouge-worthy red gown she picked for tonight. I wait with her and give her the lowdown on the men—everything I know from the two-minute walk here plus a firmness evaluation of their asses—as she does her makeup. She looks, of course, gorgeous in the dress. It has a sweetheart neckline and super-clingy sparkling silk that showcase her curves. And her hair is in this beautiful spiraling braid. Besides being blinded by her own sequins, she seems ready to go. "I'm nervous. Excited. Nervous-excited!" she squeals.

Makeup takes her at least another half hour. I'm hoping that's enough time for the guys.

Just as Heather's getting ready antsy about heading out, I get a buzz on my phone from one of the waitstaff. The men have arrived. Perfect. I escort Heather to the main dining hall.

I peer through the window. Heather, of course, can't wait

and does, too. "Oh my God. I can't believe this is actually happening." She squeezes my hand.

I smile at her. "It's actually happening. And it's going to be amazing!"

She tears up a bit. "I know this is kinda crazy, Katie. But, thank you for doing this."

I pull her into a hug. "Don't you dare cry and ruin that makeup before we start!" I scold. But I hold her close for a minute. "I love you, H."

"Love you, too."

I hear a sniffle. "I said no crying!"

"I can't help it!"

"Yes, you can. There's a motherfuckin' set of twins in there who sound like they're experts at threesomes. So get it together!"

Her jaw drops. Her fists clench. She squeals. "For reals?"

I nod.

She lamaze breathes for a moment, then nods at me. I head over to a side door where the DJ is located and awaiting my signal.

The guys are already seated, glasses of champagne in hand, and I see that an extra chair has been added to accommodate the new twin. Low mood music plays, some kind of classical classy shit. I give the DJ a head nod and he drops the music. A spotlight goes up on the main door, which two servers dramatically open to showcase Heather.

The DJ gives me a smirk and says the line Heather insisted on. "Guys, let's raise our glasses to Heather. She fell from heaven so she could be here tonight and raise some hell."

Yup, that's my girl.

THREE DRINKS LATER, my girl has sat on the laps of three different guys, failed to eat a single course, and is drunkenly giggling over something Twin One said.

She starts telling a story about the time she was cutting a guy's hair only to realize he was jerking off underneath the cape.

"What'd you do?" the guy across from her, whose profile I memorized as Peter the mechanic, asks. He's cute, in an understated way, kinda like Channing Tatum would be if he weren't stacked with muscle. Unfortunately for Peter the mechanic, he's not crazy ripped like some of the other guys here.

Heather repeats the epic throwdown she gave to Mr. Boner. "I told him, I know you love petting man's best friend there, but let me tell you, if you don't leash the beast, my scissors *will* snip him."

Laughter erupts around the table.

Down at the end of the table, a lanky Hispanic guy says, "That's nothing. At my warehouse, two guys got caught fucking."

Everyone does one of those head turns where they look silently at the person speaking because his timing sucks.

"Yeah, what happened?" Heather asks.

"They got fired!" the guy responds.

Right. Okay dude. That's not a punchline. Awkward laughs ensue.

Heather's response is, "That sucks balls—probably not as much as they did, though." She winks and the laughs resume.

She tosses me a look and I give a nod. Hispanic dude, I think his name is Gilbert, just got a strike. Three and he's out.

I toss a note in my phone and as everyone at the table goes back to chatting, I tune the conversation out and start thinking—I need to double check the room for the next event, I need to set up my projector soon, then I scheme ways to get the twins to wear identification bracelets so I can tell who's who. I'm deep in thought and don't notice as Kenneth comes in through a side door and sidles up to me, until he practically whisper-shouts in my ear.

"Why the fuck does someone order a dinner party and then not eat? If she wanted this evening to be just drunken fucking, they could have done that back in the villas."

My eyes widen. One of the guys at the table—I think it might be the doctor I was hoping would catch Heather's eye—turns to look at us.

"What?" I whisper.

Kenneth jabs an accusatory finger at Heather. "She's sent every plate back. *Untouched.*"

He's very dramatic about that 'untouched' bit. He's looking very dramatic in general. His brown eyes glitter intensely in the blue mood lighting the DJ has set. His chef's outfit almost glows, it's so white and pristine, even after cooking a five-course meal. His jaw clenches and he crosses his arms as he eyes Heather. He looks fit to be tied. In another guy, anger might scare me. But Kenneth's literally pouting because someone isn't eating his food. It's kind of cute.

I don't tell him that. But I do have to fight a smile.

"Why did I bother making a dessert? No one's going to touch it." Kenneth gets a little louder and another of the guys looks over.

Alright. Pouting has lost its cuteness. Now, he's an employee making a scene. I give the guys a fake smile, grab Kenneth's arm, and say, "Can we chat, please?" If I was my mother, my tone would be acidic face-melting bitch. But, because I'm me, this came out sounding like I'm begging. I swallow my annoyance at myself and slide my hand down Kenneth's thick, corded forearm.

His eyes dilate as my fingers trace down his palm. I can't tell if it's anger or attraction that makes his expression change. But the intensity he's radiating ratchets up, and suddenly my heart is racing. My thoughts go fuzzy. Shit. Something about Kenneth sets me off. He looks so disarming. So cuddly. Even when he's pissed as all get out. But then when he gets close, it's like a flip switches off in my brain. My thoughts are disconnected. And a whole different circuit lights up. Down there. I have to remind myself what I'm doing. I'm trying to diffuse his anger and get him out of here. I swallow hard. I nearly link fingers with him but stop myself at the last second. That would be totally unprofessional. Not cool of me. I pull him by the wrist instead, marching out into the hall.

He follows along so closely that when I stop, he bumps into me. He doesn't back up immediately, so I step away and turn to face him.

"Chef, your job is to cook—"

"Create. I don't cook. I create. Cooking is for those who follow recipes," Kenneth sneers.

Did I just think his pouting was cute? I must have been light-headed. I must be dehydrated and delusional. Because it's not cute. He's an arrogant shit. But I have to shut him up without him spitting in or spoiling our food for the next three weeks. "Well, Kenneth, your creations are amazing, but

"You didn't even try a bite."

I gesture back at the dining room. "I'm working."

"You don't need to be in there. You're standing around like a wallflower."

Wallflower is a horrible choice of words. It immediately hits me where it hurts. I try to rationalize with myself that he didn't mean I *am* a wallflower. But the old wound rips open and feelings that I've tried to suppress spill out. I mean, yeah, I'm the quiet one. Always have been. Heather's always gotten all the attention. Good or bad— from my experience watching her, mostly bad attention. But... it doesn't mean that sometimes I don't wish things were different. It doesn't mean I want to be called out on being bland, boring, plain, dull, quiet in comparison to technicolor Heather. Or anyone. I take a breath and shove those stupid feelings where they belong—into the abyss. I glare at him. "There's no need to sink to insults."

Kenneth—like every man on the planet—seems oblivious about what he just said. He's too wrapped up in himself to notice, "I spent six hours on that—"

"You spent six hours doing your job."

"If I wanted a job cooking then I'd work at Lonny's Diner back in my hometown. This isn't a job. This is art.

Haven't you ever heard the quote, 'Food is symbolic of love when words are inadequate?' —Wolfelt."

I shake my head, "Nope." That's obviously the wrong answer. I will never tell him that my childhood idea of gourmet was burgers and my adult idea of gourmet is the chain restaurant Mongolian barbeque deal down the road.

"Why hire a chef if all you want is fucking hot Cheetos?" he snarls.

Fuck! He's too loud. He's furious and aggressive and his stupid anger is echoing in the hallway. I walk toward the kitchen, hoping he'll follow.

Luckily, he does. He's not done raging at me.

I push open the door a little harder than I need to and stop short when I see tiramisu. Yum. My mouth waters just thinking about it. I haven't had dinner and my stomach grumbles. "Well, she'll eat dessert, I can promise you that. If it was me, I'd eat only that dessert."

Kenneth crosses his arms over his chest. I don't think he believes me. "You like tiramisu?"

"Love anything coffee-flavored. Coffee cake, chocolate-covered coffee beans..." I shrug. I don't mention that the Mongolian barbeque place back home, with it's completely authentic menu, serves little tiny pieces of tiramisu for dessert.

For whatever reason, my admission calms Kenneth and

he crosses over to a plate and picks it up. He grabs a spoon and walks toward me. "Prove it." He scoops a bite of the decadent treat onto the spoon and holds it up to my mouth. I reach for the spoon handle, but he jerks it away. "No."

I protest, "I can feed myself."

"Not in my kitchen."

"That's a stupid rule."

"No, it's not," he says as he steps even closer. "I never let beautiful women feed themselves in here. If I did, I wouldn't get to stand this close and watch their faces as they swallow what I've made," his voice gets breathy.

My stomach flutters at the fact that he calls me beautiful. But then I realize he just lumped me in with other women—probably lots of supermodels or plastic trophy wives. And I cringe a little when I think about what he might have 'fed' them. "You do mean food, right? Because otherwise, I'm sending a cleaning crew in here to re-bleach this room."

He laughs softly. "Ah, so there is a little fire hidden in you."

"A little," I admit. He waves the spoon in front of me and I open my mouth. He slides in the most decadent dessert I've ever tasted. I can't help the moan that escapes. It's so good, rich and creamy and thick …

"Describe it," Kenneth's thigh slides between my legs as

he scoops another bite onto a spoon. He teases me with it. "You did a great job earlier with the candy. If you tell me … I'll let you have more." He takes that bite for himself, using the spoon he just fed me with, dragging it down over his lips. My eyes end up locked on his lips as his tongue darts out and licks away the remaining cream on the spoon. His very pointed, quite flexible tongue, swirls around on the spoon, gathering up the last of the tiramisu. "Mmm. Don't you want more?" he asks.

I'm engulfed by a tropical heatwave—the sexy kind. The humidity in my pussy is like one hundred and ten percent. I want more. I do. The very feral cat-in-heat inside me wants *way* more than tiramisu. That part of me is whispering about all the things his tongue could do to me. I lean closer and closer to Kenneth's spoon.

But the timer on my watch buzzes and I look at it to see a notification. "Shit. It's almost time for Naked Friendships. Oops, nope that's tomorrow night. I mean interviews."

Kenneth's eyes crinkle at the edges as he smiles. "Naked Friendships? Is that what they call it in Oklahoma?"

I glance up and smile at him, eyes gleaming. "Depends on what you mean by *it*."

"Well, now I'm curious."

"Stop by the pool tomorrow if you want to find out." I wink and then dart out of the kitchen waving and calling out, "Thanks for the tiramisu! It tasted like a naughty dream!" Crap. I scold myself as I round the corner. I shouldn't play around with the staff like that. Dammit. But there's something about Kenneth and his weird obsession with food. He kind of reminds me of this guitar player I once knew, who'd strum the same chords over and over, obsessing over a song, sniping at everyone else who made the slightest noise around him. He was serious. He was an 'artist.'

Well, based on those candies and that tiramisu and his attitude, Kenneth is definitely an artist. The problem with artists? They're half-genius and half-crazy. And you never know which side the coin's gonna land on. Even as hot and bothered as I'm feeling, it's better to stay far, far away.

CHAPTER TEN

After dinner that first night, each of the guys gets a chance to speak privately with Heather in a room adjoining the dining room. I go double check the set up before she comes in. There's a chaise lounge in red, a few open bottles of champagne, a pitcher of water, and a lot of glasses. I take a deep breath.

Dinner was easy. Now, I get to wait outside the door and listen for Heather's safety sentence. Not just a safety word, since who knows what might come up in conversation. If any of the guys turns out to be a nut job, he can just jet back home. We decided on, "Well, aren't you cute as a button?" It's one of my mom's favorite derogatory sayings—at least when she's addressing us.

Heather clasps my hand right before she goes in. "Dinner was awesome! I can't believe this is actually happening!"

"Me either," I whisper. "You ready?"

She nods and gives a tiny squeal, then heads in.

I go collect the first guy. I enter the dining room and every male head turns to look at me. "Just me gentlemen. Coming to collect you. For those of you who are stuck waiting," I hit a button and a screen descends from the ceiling, "I have a compilation of some of Heather's greatest hits here. She's gonna ask you some questions to get to know you tonight. So, I thought it only fair you get to know her, too."

I press play. Up come the photos I have of Heather from elementary school. Her parents only saved a few. But I scanned a gem of her screaming at the school photographer. It's been the background on my phone for ages. The guys chuckle when they see it.

I move on to my list. I call the first name. "Peter Brown."

A man stands and follows me. He's the Channing Tatum lookalike I picked because Heather used to have a major crush. So, hopefully, he works out because I saw her eye him a couple times during dinner. He gives me a smile before he strides in and accepts a glass of champagne from Heather. I shut the doors behind them and stand in the hallway, feeling like a dope. Or maybe one of those British soldiers with the black cotton-ball looking hats. I wonder if they feel like dopes, standing outside rooms all day. Maybe. Of course, the rooms they stand outside aren't likely to have conversations within that focus on the question: "Why do you want to be part of a harem?"

Peter's interview seems to go well. I watch the clock to keep it to ten minutes ... gotta be fair to everyone. I lean in with my ear to the crack at the door just in time to hear, "Well, I like ass sex. And most girls don't. But I figure someone who's up for sex with multiple guys ..." he trails off.

I stifle a giggle. Then I knock, signaling that time's up. I open the door, put on my professional face, and wave my hand toward the hallway to let Peter Brown know his time has ended.

He saunters off with a wink and I tell Heather, "I'll be right back with the next 'contestant.'"

She nervous laughs. "Did you hear any of what he said?"

I grin. "The ass-sex bit, you mean?"

She busts up laughing. "Yeah. At least he was honest, I guess. He bet he could talk me into it."

"Come on, Heather! You know you're thinking about it now."

"I dunno."

"You might like it. You might love it!"

She bites her lip. "I never let Shane Paul go there."

"Don't be a pussy!"

She looks me dead on and says, "That's *exactly* the issue!"

I leave her, laughing the whole way to the dining room. I have a feeling that this entire trip is gonna be surreal.

I spy on the other interviews, curious about why each guy is interested in being one of many.

BJ from Brooklyn says he's bad with emotional stuff, so he figures he's better off letting some other guy handle it. I roll my eyes at that.

Some guys say they've always wanted a best friend to hang out with whose girlfriend isn't a barrier but a bond. (I'm pretty sure those answers are rehearsed.) My doctor pick, Andrew, says he knows his surgery schedule is going to be intense, so he figured this was fairer than a traditional relationship. We haven't decided on gold stars in our ranking system (only strikes) but I'd totally give him a star for that answer.

After his interview with Heather, as I'm escorting him back to the other guys, Anthony Drake (aka the blondie) asks me, "So what kind of stuff does Heather like?"

"The slideshow didn't tell you enough?" I ask.

He shrugs. "It was silly. Silly faces and little pranks. Flashing the cop was funny. Awful high school hair. But who doesn't have that? What's she really like?"

I keep my answer generic, favorite TV shows and whatnot. But I am somewhat impressed that he asked. Until he says, "That's all pretty normal, too. Hmm."

What a fucking weird thing to say. Like did he expect her

to be a weirdo because she wants a harem? Why sign up?
I furrow my brow "I don't know what to say to that."

But when Jeremiah Bible goes in and confesses he writes
backward poetry because he writes poems about people
who stole time, that takes the cake. Heather thinks that's
funny. I think that's borderline psychotic. But I think
chihuahuas are borderline psychotic too, and plenty of
people like them. Backwards poetry does not get a strike.

The interviews take two hours and afterward, we are all
exhausted. I dismiss the guys before I go grab Heather.

Heather punches me in the arm for the slideshow once
we're alone. "I can't believe you did that!" she says. "You
let everyone see me with crimped hair!"

"You hired a liar and docked my pay five grand!"

Her eyes narrow. "So now we're even?"

"Nope." I leave her at her door and start to trek toward
my own villa.

She calls out after me into the darkness. "We are totally
even! I had good intentions: helping you grow!"

I just yell over my shoulder. "I had good intentions,
letting these guys know what they're in for."

"Bitch!"

"Double bitch!"

She laughs, "Fine. Night!"

"Night!"

Everyone's allowed to sleep in and explore the island on day two to let the jet-lag recovery commence. But that night is an event Heather insisted on.

Naked Friendships is incredibly awkward to watch. Like watching porn with my sister. Um, no. I stare anywhere but at the guys as they roam around the pool in the buff. While we were researching events online, Heather stumbled across this tradition in Japan where people go to hot springs naked with people of the same gender. Supposedly, being naked removes inhibitions and people love it. They just bond with strangers, quickly. Heather thought it would be the perfect opener for the guys to get to know one another.

"Think about it, Katie," she'd whined, when at first, I'd said hell-to-the-no. "In all those harem books, the guys are usually BFF beforehand. Like, they know and trust each other and know what's gonna happen. My guys don't have that advantage. We need to help them bond. Fast."

And what happens when Heather wants her way? I cave.

So now, Heather's back at her villa, all the guys are nude and strolling around the pool with one poor waitstaff dude serving drinks—and me, standing off to the side awkwardly answering questions and drinking a little too much.

My announcement when the guys came out was brief.

"Drop your trunks, enjoy the drinks, and get your bromance on."

The waiter had looked over at me, alarmed.

I'd clarified, "I mean that in a very platonic way."

A couple of the guys had chuckled. One of them, a guy with beautiful eyelashes—Tim maybe? —had looked slightly disappointed.

I'd continued, "Heather wants you guys to be best friends. So, tonight, this is your locker room and y'all are free to guy it up. Apparently, there's an online article that claims doing it nude is better. So, you know … if you read it online …"

No one argued. Not a' one. They all took a couple shots and dropped trow. Now, they're mingling.

Kenneth stops by and takes one look at this event and whispers to me, "Thought this wasn't a sex cult. You needa' get the staff to bleach those chairs!" before he storms back to his kitchen, or dungeon, or 'art studio'— whatever he calls it. I stare after him longingly, kind of wishing there was someone else to suffer through this with me.

Because … awkward. I debate leaving but then a couple of the guys start arguing about sports. I don't want things to get out of hand. So, I linger. Gilbert, the guy who told the crap warehouse story earlier, can't help one-upping everyone else every time they talk. "Yeah, well the injuries our quarterback got last season were way worse."

Andrew—the doctor I picked—ignores Gilbert and asks, "Anyone watch the new documentary with those walruses that climb cliffs to avoid people?"

His question is glossed over as someone else brings up the lack of boobs on the new hit show *Striptease*.

I spot Heather crouched in the bushes, hiding and eyeing the man-candy. While she said she was gonna let the guys bond without her interference, I'm totally not surprised she's spying. My phone buzzes with a text. It's from her.

You see Peter Brown's skinny dick? No wonder he likes butt sex.

Not looking.

I don't look, but I can hear Peter Brown trying to get another guy to make a bet about which guys will make it through and end up in the harem. I roll my eyes.

My phone buzzes again. *Ohh—look at this one!*

I open the next text to see a dick pick and an *X*.

Bitch! She's fucking giving a guy a strike for his dick! I care way less about that shallow strike than the fact that she only sent me a picture of the dick and not his face. I've been studiously avoiding looking down there ... because this is not *my* sausage fest. Ugh.

Who is it? I text.

She does not respond. And I just know it's on purpose. Motherfucking traitor. She's trying to force me to eye their junk.

Not doing it, I text.

No response.

You have to tell me a name if you really want a strike, I text.

No response.

Curiosity paws at me like a kitten batting at yarn. My will unravels thread by thread. As does my professionalism. I mean, eleven yoked, naked guys are lounging around laughing.

The twins finally got some drunken takers and have started up a chicken fight and there's a lot of hot male on male riding and splashing going on. What woman could resist?

I open the text again to check the penis in question. It's long, so probably a 'show'-er, not a grower. But it's thin. And—eww, eww, eww—it's uncircumcised. That's been a thing for Heather since we started talking about sex. There are things that float your boat and things that make it sink. To Heather, uncircumcised weenies are shipwrecks.

My eyes flicker up to see who might have the little love

warrior wearing a helmet. Even as my eyes slide up, my heart starts hammering. I do not want to get called out for eyeing the goods. Subtle. Subtle. Professional face. Keep on a professional face.

I scan the guys standing by the bar. One, two, three—not it. I let out the breath I've been holding with a *whoosh*. I glance back at my phone and pretend I'm doing something important. My fingers tap away like I'm sending a message. Really, I'm just typing XXXXX into my phone. I'm a super spy. It's what I tell myself to keep going, even though my stomach is roiling. Fuck. I fucking arranged this naked time. I shouldn't be nervous, right? But dammit, that was before. I didn't think I'd end up having to secretly ogle. I should have had them all put dick pics in their files.

My eyes slide toward the waterfall. I can't fucking see clearly around the little splashes and mist the waterfall makes. Shit.

I look at the guys in the lounge chairs, heart hammering. One of the guys, Karl Nork (a former military man and a hottie who's got this amazing nose that gives him this lion, alpha-predator feel) makes eye contact with me and I give him a professional nod and then go back to typing on my phone, trying to ignore the raging blush that takes over my entire face.

When I glance up again, Nork isn't in his seat anymore. Fuck! Did he realize what I was doing? Is he telling people? Crap! I'm gonna end up being the creeper lady.

I'm gonna have to resign and find someone else to run this gig. I'm gonna be the first person Alec flies out of here. The thought of being on a plane alone with Alec only doubles my blush.

Karl Nork is suddenly in front of me. All five foot eleven, naked, muscled goodness.

Busted.

My mouth is suddenly as dry as sex without foreplay. And this moment feels just about as bad, too. Painfully uncomfortable. All I can think about is how I wish I wasn't here right now. I want a body swap. Any body swap. I don't even care. I just don't want to be me right now. Crap!!! My eyes have trouble meeting Karl's. He's gonna call me on it. I just know he's gonna call me on the staring. An uncomfortable laugh starts and I clench my teeth together to stop it.

Karl's eyes study mine for a long second before he holds up his cell and asks, "What's the wifi password?"

If I was a kite, I'd crash into a tree right now. His question makes all the tension holding my body taut just stop dead. Like a wind that just disappears without rhyme or reason. My resulting smile is far too wide for the question, but little does he know, it's a smile of relief and not just a fake, little professional showing-of-the-teeth.

My fake hostess voice clicks on automatically. "Sure. It's island222, all lowercase."

He types it into his phone and smiles. "Awesome." He turns and I cannot believe my luck.

Until he turns back.

"By the way, in case you're wondering, I'm just over six inches when hard, a good four inches in girth. Heather's having you send the details, right?"

Caspar's got nothing on me. My face is white as a sheet. I'm pretty sure I've just died, too. Half from humor, half from humiliation. I don't have it in me to respond. I just stare blankly at him.

He winks and walks off.

I deflate. Gah! Weddings are not this stressful. Angry mothers-of-the-bride are not half as bad as spying on nudie-patootie men. I am all out of energy after that tension. If there was a couch behind me, I'd totally sink into it. As it is, I just take off my heels. I'm done. Officially done for the night. One more tense moment and my heart's gonna explode.

I pick my heels up. Heather can just deal with the foreskin dude. I'm not giving anyone an X for that. Especially if she can't give me a name.

I straighten up, heels in hand, about to tell the guys that they should turn in during the next hour or so because we've got a busy day tomorrow. But before I can speak, there's a crunch, right in my ear. I jump a little. I turn to see Danny Walsh, liar and supposed tennis player, standing next to me, eating a bag of chips and staring without shame at the naked frolicking. A couple more guys are in the pool now, and the twins are really trying to convince them to join in the chicken fighting.

"So, this is weird," Danny comments conversationally.

"Give me a chip," I grouse, reaching for his bag.

He lets me dig in and I'm thrilled to find he's eating my favorite flavor. Vinegar. "Mmm."

Several guys turn their heads and I wave my hands while staring up at the palm trees. "The chips. Not you. The chips. I wasn't looking!"

Danny chuckles beside me and calls out, "She means she doesn't want to admit she was looking!"

That earns a laugh and I turn as red as a boiled lobster.

"Lie," I mutter.

"No, it's not," Danny grins and stuffs another chip in his too handsome mouth. If only he knew.

I glare at him and grab the chip bag away. "I'm starving. I didn't have dinner. Where'd you get the chips?"

"Not from the kitchen that's for sure," Danny grumbles. "If I'd have known that coming here would mean I'd be on a five-star diet, I would have packed a gym bag full of junk food."

"You don't like the food?" Damn, I'm glad Kenneth went back inside. He'd have a conniption.

"I asked that Kenneth guy for a snack and he made me a beet salad." Danny snorts. "That's not a fucking snack."

"How old are you?"

"Twenty-four."

No wonder he's so hot. All twenty-four-year olds... he lifts the chip bag and pours some chips into his mouth and his six-pack peeks out at me again. Okay, nope. Not all twenty-four-year olds are that hot. But only twenty-four year olds can eat like that and still be hot. I swipe the chip bag back before he can finish it off. Three fucking chips left. I eat two and hand over the last grumpily, wishing for more.

I ask, "The golf course doesn't have a vending machine?"

He shakes his head. "They don't even have regular water over there. Seltzer. That kind in the green bottle. Blech."

I glance at him, evaluating as Danny stares unabashedly at the twins, who are demonstrating how to play naked chicken without their junk dangling all over the guy in front of them, which involves a very precarious balancing situation.

My eyes roam over Danny's classic American good-boy features. The seltzer comment was unusually specific. I think back to the story about his brother's 'car accident.'

There were a lot of details in that, too. I form a theory as I watch his square jaw crunch down on the last chip.

"Where'd you get the chips?" I ask.

"Had one bag in my stuff. Must have thrown it in there when I was packing."

I hazard a guess, "Lie!"

He turns to me, eyes wide. "No! It's not!"

But there's a panic in his tone that makes me suspect I'm right. That there are normal snacks somewhere. And he's hoarding them.

I bolt toward the golf course. It's a nine-hole course set back a bit from the villas. I run until I realize Danny isn't following me. He's not trying to stop me. That realization makes me slow down.

He double-lied. He knew I'd think he was lying ... so like any good con man, he offered up a red herring.

Fuck me.

I think hard and I remember the last time I saw Danny eating chips. It was on the plane.

I hoof it over to the tarmac. If my horny ass is gonna have to work while watching nearly a dozen dudes try and get with my bestie then I'm gonna need a shit ton of junk food to cope.

CHAPTER ELEVEN

The door to the plane is firmly shut. I smack on the side, but the crash of the ocean waves next to the runway is louder than my puny smacks. There are directions on the door about how to open it properly, but they are hard to read by starlight. Plus, it's a door. You pull the handle. I pull the handle and *wham!* The door falls straight down—fast—smacking me in the shoulder.

"Ahh!" I scream, scrambling out of the way and clutching my shoulder. My entire arm instantly pulses with hot pain. That door was fucking heavy.

Alec appears in the doorway of the plane. "Katie?"

I don't respond. I'm too busy moaning and cursing my stupidity for wanting goddamn chips.

Alec descends the stairs connected to the inside of the door and comes over. He touches my lower back, and despite the pain, the touch has me looking up through my tears to stare into his eyes.

His brow is creased in concern. "Can you move your hand? Anything broken?"

I just groan.

He slides his hand up my back, and the throbbing heat in my shoulder is in stark contrast to the shiver that trails up my spine at his touch.

"I'm going to check, okay? Just stay still." His fingers slide up along my neck and then slowly down my arm. I'm sore, and tender, but nothing he does causes shooting pain. I'm more fascinated by how tender he is, and how intent his deep brown eyes are as they study my arm.

"You look like you know what you're doing."

A tiny grin cracks on his lips. "Broken a few bones in my time."

I smile, "Okay, grandpa."

His eyes narrow on me. "Watch that lip, whippersnapper." Then he winks. "I think you're fine. But you definitely need ice because otherwise you're gonna end up looking like a hunchback."

"That'll match my witch nose perfectly," I say with a grin.

"Witch nose? Nah, your nose is cute. Not as good as your smile, but..." he trails off, suddenly shy.

I swallow hard. He likes my smile? I get a bit lightheaded. And I don't think it's from my injury.

Alec holds out his arm. "Let me help you get on the plane and we'll get you that ice."

I use the excuse to clutch at his bicep with my good hand. Whoa. He's thick and hard as stone. My shoulder suddenly isn't the only thing pulsing with painful heat.

Alec helps me up the stairs and deposits me in one of the white leather seats. He goes to the drink station and builds an improvised icepack. He looks over his shoulder at me as he does and asks, "So, why are you out here in the middle of the night?"

Because I'm in pain and it makes me feel better to blame someone else for my stupidity, I say, "Danny lied to me."

Alec's expression immediately hardens. "You and ..." He shakes his head as he trails off. Instead, he asks a different question as he walks over and hands me my icepack. "And that made you come out here because ... you want me to fly you home?"

I start to shake my head, but pain stabs my neck. So, I plop the icepack on top of my shoulder and say, "Nope. He tried to hide the fact that there are chips on this plane."

Alec takes the seat directly across from me and laughs. "Chips? He lied about chips."

"Chips are important."

"So important that you came running down here at midnight."

"I was worried he'd take them all for himself."

"He did."

"What?" I lean forward in my seat.

Alec bites his lip and shrugs. "He'd literally just left with a duffel bag full of plane snacks, asking me to re-up when I go elsewhere."

"Fucker!" The curse is out of my mouth before I can stop it. But Mom's ingrained manners have me immediately apologizing. "Sorry. That was rude of me. I'm just annoyed, is all. There is apparently no junk food on this island."

He leans back in his seat and stretches out his legs, clearly entertained. "Curse away. I was in the air force. Doubt you could say anything I haven't heard."

I purse my lips and think for a second. "Cuntasaurus. Twatapotamus."

He busts out laughing. "What the fuck?! What are those?"

"My secret favorite names for Heather behind her back. Though now, I'm pretty sure they apply to Danny Walsh, liar and chip-stealer."

He shakes his head. "You guys must be really close."

"Heather and I grew up together. She lived with my family after her parents died."

He nods. "And Danny? You guys…"

A thrill runs through me and I lean forward a little further. "You fishing?"

Alec's breath hitches. "Maybe."

My stomach feels light and airy. Almost ticklish inside. I swallow a giddy giggle. Alec is so freaking hot. And he's fishing for info about me and Danny. Which means he might, possibly, maybe … be interested in me. His brown eyes don't leave mine as I smile slowly. "I only met Danny Walsh once before this trip. Heather hired him to try to make me more confrontational. Plus, I guess he's good at sports or something," I wave my good hand dismissively.

"Confrontational? The woman who researches donkey sex revenge isn't confrontational?" Alec grins and leans forward on with his elbows on his knees. That puts his face only inches from mine. I can see the throb of his pulse in his neck, every hair in the scruff from his two-day beard. I can see his nostrils flare as he inhales scent of the tropical pineapple lotion I put on.

I lick my lips and a nervous giggle escapes. "Only in my head. And in real life, really only with Heather."

"Why?" I can smell a hint of mint on his breath when he asks.

"I get uncomfortable when people are mad at me. Or other people. I just hate—tension," I confess as I shift the icepack further down my shoulder.

"Not with her?"

I shrug. "If I don't snap sometimes at her, she'll railroad me. She's wild. She wanted us to get tattoos."

"You're the good girl."

I narrow my eyes and point a finger at him. "I resent that."

Alec raises his eyebrow and chuckles. "I guess I'm more of a Heather. Or kind of. I used to live for tension, adrenaline, riding the edge. Was a fighter pilot when I was younger."

"Yeah?" I can see that. Alec's rock-hard muscles are a testament to his hard work and training, and the fact that he flies for rich ass people—he must have been the best because that's what his frickin' price per flight hour buys —the best. "Why'd you stop?"

Alec's eyes search mine. "Excitement is only fulfilling for a while. I started to want something more."

"What?"

He bites his lip. "Not sure. I haven't found it yet."

Fuck. Something about that just rings so fucking true to me. It's so real, and honest, and raw. And I feel the exact same way. I'm thirty fucking years old and I have no idea what the fuck my life is supposed to be about. I've been biding my time at the dental office, just shuffling through the days, waiting. For something. A sign. A bright fucking neon sign that says "Hey Katie! Life's purpose is here. Right here! Come and get it!" The connection I've been feeling with Alec, the tingling sexual attraction, solidifies into something more. Something better. And that's why my lips go crashing into his.

His lips are perfect. Thick and strong as they move against mine. His tongue shoots out into my mouth and I whimper. Then our tongues tangle together, in a hot wet precursor to other hot wet things. I move from my chair to straddle his legs and sit down on him. His hands slide around my waist. His fingers dig into my ass. He growls into my neck and the animalistic sound drives me wild.

It feels like my fingers are tripping over themselves as I undo his buttons, I am that eager to get his shirt off.

When his mouth leaves my lips I whine in protest, but when it locks onto the sensitive skin of my neck below my ear, I arch into him, his shirt temporarily forgotten.

"Yes! There!" I moan.

"You're so sweet."

His hands trace the crack of my ass through my suit skirt, which had gotten hiked up when I sat. I drag the hem of my skirt up further, the sensation titillating my hips. I move his hands to my panties, loving the rough feel of his fingers on my skin. He starts to play with the bottom edge of my lacy panties, sneaking his fingertips under the hem every so often, which just makes me grind into his erection harder.

Fuck. I've needed this. So bad. This hot, mindless hunger. I've needed to burn off steam.

My hands resume their task. I'm eager to get Alec naked, to have his fingers go further than the edges of my underwear, to have him ride me.

His erection is thick and long in his pants, and I can tell just by the rub of it against my thighs that he's bigger than any man I'd ever been with. That's both intimidating and exciting. After I finish with the shirt buttons and slide his shirt down his shoulders. I wrap my arms around Alec's back and pull myself further onto him so that I can better grind down onto the hot, hard length of him.

"I want you," I whisper. "I want you to hold me down and slam into me—"

Alec growls and freezes. I stare at his eyes for a second. I see panic cross his features the second before he shoves me backward, off his legs. I stumble into the seat behind me and end up windmilling so I don't fall on my ass.

"What the fuck?" I ask.

Alec pulls his shirt back on, leans his elbows onto his knees and covers his face with his hands. He's breathing hard.

I stand there, staring at him, wondering what the hell I just did, what the hell just went wrong.

Alec doesn't tell me. He just bolts past me, down the aisle, and out the door.

I'm left horny, on a plane, in the middle of the night on a tropical island.

I take a deep breath, lay down on the floor, and stare up at the ceiling. I'm on an island filled with guys who signed up to walk around naked together and have group sexy times with Heather ... and I can't even get one hot guy to fuck me?

I toss my hand up in the air and flip the universe the bird.

Then I go back to the villas and use my universal key to sneak into Danny's room and steal that sleeping mother-fucker's snacks.

CHAPTER TWELVE

I hardly see Alec over the next few days, which is just fine by me. I'm still pissed at him. So pissed I almost attacked Danny the liar in his bed that night and woke him by riding his cock. Oh, I thought about it. Danny looked like a damned magazine picture with his blond hair falling over his eyes. But I chose Cheetos. They'd be there for me rain or shine. Men? Not so much.

Alec's only near me when I have to escort Heather and small groups of guys over to the jet for group dates. The island we rented is too small for some things. Like a full game of golf. We only have a nine-hole course. So, the first morning after the plane crash—as I started calling the incident—I escort Heather and three of her men to the runway so they can jet over to a nearby island for eighteen holes.

Alec tries to pull me aside. He has that 'we should talk'

look on his face, but I just wrench my arm away, fake laugh, and avoid direct eye contact.

"Well, now you guys be good! Have fun! Take pictures!" I call as I walk quickly away. He can reject me if he wants. But no way we're talking about it all friendly-like.

BJ, a New Yorker with an accent and a crooked nose, winkes when I got back from delivering Heather. "Who do ya think might use their wood on the first hole?"

The other guys crack up and the golf jokes ensued. I never knew there were so many. BJ has the most for some reason, maybe because his roommate is on the date.

"Yeah, bet Karl will work his stroke out there. Hope he doesn't hit that so hard he bends his shaft!"

"Could you blame him? First date is a foursome. That's a good fucking date!" Jeremiah Bible jokes. My random last-minute pick has kept a low profile so far. He's handsome, but not too much. Outspoken, but not too much. I worry a bit about him fading into the background.

He's not my absolute favorite, I sent Andrew (my doctor pick) on the first date, but I decide to pull him aside and give him a little help anyway.

"Think they'll stop and wash their balls after?" one of the twins asks.

"Think those guys will share clubs?" Twin Two wonders.

Finally, I can jump in on the jokes. "If they do, Heather might get tee'd off."

It's like someone's turned down the volume on the laughter. Polite titters ensue when the guys realize I'm a woman and still standing there as they make sports jokes. I want to blow a raspberry. But instead I fake smile and touch Jeremiah's arm. "Walk with me?"

"Sure," he sets down his water cup and we go off onto a path that leads toward the tennis courts.

"So, I've noticed you're pretty quiet," I say.

Jeremiah clears his throat and I realize there's a bit of a gap between his front teeth. He could do with some invisalign. "I do better in smaller groups."

I nod. "Well, you're on the jungle tour date tomorrow with Heather, so that should help. My goal is just to make sure all of you are comfortable."

"I'm comfortable," he insists way too quickly. "I adapt to all kinda situations. My dad's a prepper. I just need to know what's up."

I stop walking as my wackadoo detector goes off. He stops walking. I smile at him. "If being here makes you nervous—"

"How's she got all this cash?" Jeremiah busts out. "I'm sorry. It's just, I looked this place up. It costs a shit-ton to be here. I've never been around someone with all this money and I've got ...Heather's mobster dad's gonna kill me thoughts running through my head. I just wanna know so I can prepare."

I laugh so hard I snort and my hand flies to my face. "That's the best thing I've heard all day!"

Jeremiah doesn't look so happy about my laughter, so I fight to swallow it. "I'm sorry! No, nothing like that. It's her story to tell, so check with her. Not because it's dark or bad, but I literally think she might shoot me if I tell it. She loves to talk about herself."

Jeremiah nods and we go our separate ways. I don't think I've fully convinced him that Heather's not a mobster. But the idea is so funny that I order her a hat, the pinstriped kind with a feather in it, from my phone.

When Heather gets back from her group date, drama ensues, as typical of Heather. She bursts off the plane fit to be tied.

I rush over to see what's wrong. I didn't go on that date in order to give them privacy. But did the club not have golf carts? Did I order her the wrong size golf shoes? Were there not enough caddies? I asked and the resort assured me … the million reasons this could be my fault run through my head.

"You're an asshole! Total and complete!" Heather spits out at Karl. She turns to me and starts yelling, "Pea-cocking the entire time and trying to tell me how to line up a stupid putt when he can't tell a sand wedge from a nine iron. Probably can't tell a fart from a yawn either! Of course, when you're an ass, guess they're one and the same!" Oh, shit. Hurricane Heather strikes again.

I hurry forward and grab Karl by the elbow. "I guess I'll just let you pack."

He yanks his elbow out of my grip and stomps off to his villa. I blow out a deep breath and follow. I didn't think about mentioning it to the guys. But this is my fault.

Shane Paul had insisted Heather take golf lessons with him, so he'd have someone to practice with before he went on business trips. He'd even changed out a chunk of their backyard for a putting green. I really should have said something. I'm guessing Karl thought this was supposed to be a 'hands on' demonstration kind of date.

Dammit. I need to apologize to Heather.

But first, I deal with Nork. I've never been fired, but right now, I feel like I'm the HR lady walking out the crazy volatile dude who was just let go. Nork rolls his suitcase out and his face is a thundercloud. He doesn't say a word, but I cringe anyway and trot behind him instead of next to him. I worry what I'm gonna do when the next guy leaves. Because that's inevitable. I try to take deep yoga breaths: in through the nose and out through the mouth.

When Nork and I reach the jet, I open my mouth to say goodbye but just manage an awkward nod, my face burning as if I'm the one who kicked him off the island. Seeing Alec lower the plane door so Nork can climb aboard doesn't help. It makes my face burn double hot.

Fuck. And I'm pissed at myself. I stare out at the ocean waves and curse my stupid self for getting all uncomfortable because that makes Alec think he's important. And he's not. I just kissed him. It was just attraction. Not a big fucking deal at all. It wasn't anything more.

I stomp off as soon as Nork's inside the jet, not bothering to look back when Alec calls my name.

Just do your job buddy and I'll do mine.

Danny comes off a side path with his tennis racket in hand. He's whistling but he stops when he sees my face. He trots over to walk next to me and asks, "What could possibly be bumming you out in paradise?"

"Not everyone can be as happy as a pig in the sunshine, Danny," I say, stomping away from him.

He doesn't get the hint. "Maybe you've been eating too many snacks—"

I whirl on him and stick a finger under his too-straight Ken nose. "Do not call me fat!"

"Whoa! I was just gonna say maybe you spiked the blood sugar—keeping all those treats for yourself." He studies his nails.

I narrow my eyes. "You are way too calm about the fact that I stole them."

He grins. "It's cause I stole them back." He walks off, whistling.

I wish I thought he was lying. But I don't. "How?"
I ask.

"Told a maid you had a box of extra tennis balls laying
around that I needed," he turns around and walks backward down the path, smiling at me. He doesn't even have
the decency to trip like an asshole should.

"I hate you," I seethe.

His lip tilts up in a cocky grin that makes my breath
catch. He clicks his tongue and winks. "Now, that is a
lie."

I HEAD over to Heather's villa to get the deets on Karl.
But, as I arrive, I see a guy standing in her doorway,
talking to her. My feet slow to give them privacy. I stare
at the pink hibiscus flowers in front of me, instead of
spying on the two of them like a little part of me wants to
do. I hear Heather laugh. I do a mini fist pump. Good. So,
even if Karl turned into an ass, at least the date doesn't
seem like a total disaster.

A minute later, I see Anthony Drake, a real estate agent
with huge lips and a winning smile, walk past me. He
gives me his signature smile, big glowing bleached teeth. I
definitely approve of that smile. Not a hint of plaque in
sight.

"What up, Katie?"

I tilt my head toward Heather. "You get her cooled down for me?"

He puts a hand to his chest. "I'm offended you could even think that. When I speak to a lady, all I do is get her worked up."

Alrighty then. Fake smile in place, I turn and make my way to Heather. I guess some guys could pull off a line like that and be funny. But Drake just comes off as a douche. I don't get to give strikes, but I'll definitely be pointing Heather in another direction.

I knock on her door and open it before just walking in. "It's me!" I call as I step into her very posh villa.

The floors are the tile that looks like wood. The ceiling is bamboo with a huge fan rotating lazily. Floor to ceiling windows line the far wall so she can look out onto a tropical garden where parrots have been imported and trained to impress the rich vacationers with sayings like, "Cracker! No! Gimme a margarita!" I can see one of the little red fuckers now, using his beak to help him climb the balcony.

"Kay, that date was insane!" Heather comes out of her room half-dressed, golf skirt already missing. She's got zero body shame. I've always envied that. Of course, with her figure, it's easy to be proud. She's an hourglass.

Heather pulls her hair out of the high ponytail she was wearing and then yanks her shirt over her head. She walks back toward her room, still talking. "I mean, what an arrogant shit! He didn't even ask if I'd played before he started trying to pick clubs for me and shove his boner in my ass in the name of 'helping me.' Some guys ..."

I sigh and sit on her bed as she goes through twelve cute dresses before changing into a short pink sun dress. It hugs her figure in all the right ways and she pairs it with gold sandals. "At least you found out early. And you weren't alone with him."

Heather snorts. "If we'd been alone, he'd have gotten a junk punch. The other guys lined him out, though. Especially Andrew. He was really sweet." She stops with her dress halfway pulled down, a dreamy little grin on her face.

"Andrew?" I ask. "Not Anthony, the guy who was just here?"

She waves me off as she finishes her dress and goes to sit at her makeup table, which has more tools than they used to build the Vatican. Probably more paintbrushes than Michelangelo, too. Golf makeup comes off and a more flirty, pink look gets started. "No, not Anthony. That guy's a little ... different."

"You're being PC," I tell her. "You're never PC."

She shrugs into the mirror as she pops her lips to check her lipstick. "I'm not sure what's off yet, maybe we just didn't click. I've never done the group dating thing."

"Was it weird?" I'm very curious. I've never done the

group date thing. I think it might get weird in real life. Do the guys take turns? Do they have to discuss it before-hand? Work out a lineup like baseball? What if one of them gets Heather to laugh? Do the others feel jealous?

Heather's response stops my train of thought. "No, it wasn't weird, actually. It was super-fun. Like just hanging out with a group of friends." She turns to look at me, one eye full of mascara and the other eye bare. "I think naked friendships worked. We should do it again. New plan—every night is naked friendship night for the guys I'm not on a date with."

I give her a big grin. "Got it, boss. But … question. Do you worry about any of them being more into each other than you?"

She laughs. "You mean Rubin and Reval, don't you? They giving you a Lannister twin vibe?"

I nod. "But you're keeping them?"

She stares at me like I'm the crazy one. "They're twins. *Hot* twins."

I shake my head in disbelief—mostly at myself. "Far be it from me … so tell me more about Andrew, the doctor, right?" I try and keep my voice casual. No need to preen. Heather will get all uppity if she thinks that I'm better at picking guys for her than she is. But I totally am. I picked the guy prior to Shane Paul and never liked Shane Paul. And that turned out … well, it's why she's here.

Heather finishes her mascara before heading over to me. She flops down on the bed and I sit next to her, propping my back up against the headboard so I can see her better.

"So ... what was it?" I prompt.

She bites her lip and grins. It's almost a shy look, which I never fucking see from her. I grab her arm. "What?"

She shakes her head. "It's stupid. Never mind. It's just a little thing."

I grab both her shoulders and lean in. "You tell me right this instant, Heather Graham! Or I'm flying my mother down here to see what you're up to!"

Her jaw drops. "I won't pay you!"

I cross my arms smugly. "You already signed a contract. At a lawyer's office."

"I'll hire someone to run around and yell at you and make you uncomfortable all day, every day!"

I collapse back onto the headboard and laugh. "You already did that! Danny's annoying as shit!"

She giggles. "Oh yeah. I forgot. But you totally were crushing on him at that law office."

"Til I found out he's cray cray."

She shakes her head and lays back on the middle of the mattress, letting her feet dangle. "You need a little cray cray."

"No, I don't. I have you."

"Exactly! You need, like, a guy version of me!"

"You're not a liar."

She tugs her hand through her dark hair, picking out the purple peekaboos until she's got a fist full of purple hair. "Not always. But I brought Danny before I saw that pilot... damn you and he have some chemistry! You tap that?" She clicks her tongue and winks.

I shake my head big time. "Nope. Tried. Struck out. I don't do complicated."

"Just because Michael was ..."

I freeze and stare at her. My heart starts beating double time. She said his name. She said the bastard's name.

Heather actually stops what she's doing. Her eyes flicker to mine guiltily. She knows she just broke a rule. But her stupid mouth doesn't apologize. She says softly, "You've gotta move past him sometime."

And like that, a wall goes up between us. My shields slam down with the force of ballistic glass. I can see her. But she's on the outside now. We're separated. Just mentioning him with sympathy makes my hackles rise.

I stand and my tone is red hot fire. "I've moved past him. I just remember the lesson he taught me." I storm out of the bedroom.

Just as I'm about to get to her front door, Heather grabs my arm. I spin around, ready to smack her.

"Wait! Don't go. I'm sorry." She strokes my arm and her eyes are full of tears. "I'm sorry."

She slides her arms around me and gives me a hug.

It takes a minute, but slowly my posture softens. I say, "You know I don't like to talk—"

"I know. I'm sorry." She pulls back from the hug and studies my face. "Will it make it up to you a little if I tell you about Andrew?"

I shrug. "It's a start."

Heather leads me over to the modern grey couches in her living room. We sink down onto the plush cushions.

I try to shake off the bad mood that gripped me at the mention of Michael's name. "So ... you liked the guy I picked out for you."

A blush rises on her cheeks and she rolls her eyes. "I mean, this is nothing major. It's kind of ridiculous even."

"What's ridiculous?"

"We started talking pet peeves. And he and I have almost the exact same ones!"

I just scrunch my brow, waiting for more. That's cute but ... like really, how much of a connection can you have over pet peeves?

"So ... when the milk is almost out and there's an unopened container of milk in the fridge, what should you do?"

"Finish the first milk?"

"Yes!" Heather's hands clench. "Shane Paul, that fucker, would always just open the new milk. Finish it and put it in the goddamned recycling!" She shakes her head in disbelief.

"He was a heathen," I agree.

"He was. Anyway, Andrew had an ex who would do that with orange juice. Like, even up to leaving expired unfinished cartons in the fridge. He drank bad OJ once."

"Ew!" I cringe.

"Bitch! Right?" she says. "Okay, another one. Nail clippers are a good invention. People should not just fucking bite their nails off. Or, in Shane Paul's case, peel his motherfuckin' toenails off and leave them on the coffee table like god-damned dead maggots!"

I try not to laugh at her but fail. "It sounds like you have so much in common!"

She tosses a pillow at me. "Like I said. It's stupid. But ... you know, it's a start."

I grin and toss the pillow gently back to her. "That's awesome, Heath." I glance at my phone and groan. "Dammit. I gotta go check on the staff and make sure the luau pit is on track." I stand and stretch. Then I remember what I wanted to share with Heather. "Oh, guess what was funny today?"

"Huh?" She looks up from staring out the window.

I grin, guessing she's mooning over Andrew. "So, one of the guys was all worried about where the cash was coming from for this place. He thought you were some mafia princess."

Heather laughs. Hard. So hard that her laughing makes me start to laugh. We spend a couple minutes in rib-cracking laughter before she stands and walks me out. "I love it," she says. "You didn't tell him the truth?"

I shake my head and open the door. "Nah. I thought I'd let you tell him your real mobster name yourself."

"Ooh, I could be like, Heather 'Queenie' Graham."

"Heather 'Big Hair' Graham," I toss out.

"Oh, I think it needs to be more dangerous," Heather says as she pulls open her door. "I mean, I wouldn't want my mobsters to think of me as shallow."

"I think they're called associates," I bite my lip.

She raises an eyebrow. "Look at you. Getting the lingo down. We'll have you shooting people up in no time."

I turn to leave and see four guys standing outside Heather's porch holding a cake.

Jeremiah Bible, the gap-toothed dude that brought about the mafia jokes, is grinning ear to ear and giggling slightly as he holds the pink cake. BJ Cannavaro, a hot Italian guy with blue eyes, looks back and forth between Heather and me, like he wants to say something. He doesn't though. Next to him, Tim Wu gives a small smile.

Matt Rooney—a hot half-Asian guy with great hair— speaks first, "We brought a cake, for the holiday."

"Holiday?" I ask.

Jeremiah Bible can't stop himself. His laughter busts out like a tuba as he turns the cake to face us. It looks like a giant vagina. "Chef made it."

My jaw drops. Is this some kind of weird guy prank? My eyes flicker to each of the guys. But their eyes are on Heather.

Matt just raises an eyebrow and says, "Doesn't everyone celebrate April 14th? It's cake and cunnilingus day."

I book it down the path as Heather smiles and opens her door wide. I don't even care that I'm in heels. I mother-fucking run. Because that's the best fucking holiday ever. But, based on the gleam in all eyes, everyone was gonna have their cake. And their Heather, too.

CHAPTER THIRTEEN

I drop by the kitchen later to compliment Kenneth on his cuntcake skills.

He's wearing his chef uniform and a blue bandana on his forehead when I find him, which makes him look like a cross between a motorcycle gang member and Chef Boyardee.

He's pouring a hot peach-colored liquid into molds when I find him, so I stand off to the side near the pantry, not wanting to disturb him. Kenneth whispers to himself as he pours. "Come on baby, curl in there, you love it, oh yeah, just a little more. You'll fit. You'll fit. Slow, honey. We like it slow."

His little whispers sound so dirty that I can't help a giggle. Or maybe my mind's still just in the gutter from cake and cunnilingus day.

Kenneth finishes with a mold before he turns to look at me. When he sees me, a wide smile crosses his face. And I can't help the warmth that spreads through my stomach. It's like being greeted by cotton candy and summertime. Sweetness and freedom and fond memories somehow all roll together into that smile. And even though his teeth aren't quite perfectly straight, the joy in his smile just makes that imperfection a bit more endearing.

Without thinking, I find myself taking a step closer to Kenneth. When I realize what I've done, I clear my throat awkwardly.

Kenneth sets down the pan of peach-colored syrup on the stove. Then he steps toward me, slinging the towel he used as a potholder over his shoulder. "Katie. I've been thinking about you."

My entire body tingles at those words. The hairs stand up on my arms. It's a line women dream about hearing from a guy they're crushing on. But I'm a bit taken aback. Why would he be thinking about me? Our last interaction was awkward at best. And then I said that cringe-worthy line. 'It tasted like a naughty dream.' What the fuck was I thinking? I look at Kenneth nervously and ask, "You have?"

"Yes. You've been my muse. I've been trying to fix those pineapple candies you didn't like," he nods toward the molds.

"Oh," I'm so relieved he's not thinking about the other thing I said that my smile stretches wide. Maybe too wide, because suddenly he's close. And he smells delicious. Tropical, like punch or juice. I could just drink him down. I swallow hard and try to maintain eye contact instead of just pulling him into me so that I can see if he tastes as good as he smells.

"What did you add?" my voice comes out a little breathy.

He leans in further and my mind is completely overtaken by my awareness of him. The arch of his brow when he grins down at me. The glitter in his eyes. The charge in the air between us. He licks his lips and I feel his exhale trace over my cheek. My face tingles, the promise of a kiss hovering between us.

"I used passion fruit," he whispers. "I thought it was appropriate." His lips get close enough to tickle the skin of my cheek as he leans forward and whispers in my ear, "I want you to taste it. I want you to taste what I made for you."

"Okay," I have to physically restrain myself from collapsing in his arms.

Kenneth gives me a naughty, knowing smile as he backs away and takes my hand. He pulls me toward the molds he's poured. There are twelve trays, and he selects the furthest one from where I initially found him. "The texture might be a little tacky since it's still setting up, but the flavor ... it should be as delicious as those lips of yours look."

I bite down on a giggle that threatens to turn manic. Fuck! He's gotta be a player. The man knows how to compliment.

Kenneth wiggles a candy loose from the mold and says, "Open your mouth."

I comply.

He puts his fingers into my mouth and drops the candy onto my tongue. But then he uses my lips to clean each of his fingers. As he slides his thumb through my lips, my tongue traces the pad, licking every bit of stickiness off.

"What do you think?" he asks, stepping closer.

The taste is bright orange and yellow sunshine, citrusy bursts of goodness. It's exactly what I'd want to eat to take me back to this island, to make me think of tropical, exotic vacations. "It's perfect."

I only see Kenneth's smile for a second before he yanks me into his chest, shoving a leg between my thighs. "My turn to taste," he commands.

And then his lips devour mine. His teeth nip, his hands roam, and he steals the candy right from my mouth. He's Tropical Storm Kenneth and I'm caught in his wake. My head is spinning, and my heart is thudding, blown over by him. I've never felt this fucking desired in my entire life. And I love it.

My tongue gets aggressive and I steal the candy right back, sucking his tongue into my mouth in the process. That makes his hands dig into my waist and push me down on his leg. Then he starts to slide me back and forth slightly, teasing me, grinding me against his leg until I'm breathless. I'm forced to break the kiss as I gasp when he helps me rub against him just right.

"Am I driving you crazy?" he whispers.

"Yes."

"Good. You've been driving me crazy since your first night here." Kenneth nips at my lips one more time. "I wish we could keep going. But I have to start on dinner."

"That's not for four hours," I point out.

"Exactly. I don't have a lot of time." He pulls his thigh from between mine.

The selfish, immature part of me wants to clamp my legs tight and keep him there. But I don't. "You really take your job seriously."

"It's the most important thing in my life," he tells me solemnly.

I can tell it's true for him. But at the same time, it seems a little lonely to me. A little sad. "Really?"

He nods. "I've given up everything to get here. And I'm not done. I'm going to have my own restaurant one day. I have a vision."

I give him a half-smile. "It's great that you can see your future so clearly."

He stares at me for a second. "Sometimes. At the same time, I know I hurt people when I tell them they won't ever be as important as the dream." He lifts my hand and kisses the back of it. "You are a beautiful muse. But I only do sex. Are you alright with that?"

I grin. "Sex without a relationship? That's basically my MO." I wink.

He spins me into him like we're dancing. My back ends up against his chest. "You'd better be serious," he whispers in my ear. He rubs his cock against the back of my ass, and I can feel how hard he is.

Oh, thank God! I'm finally going to be able to sate this sexual need that's been nagging me, growing each day since Heather cut me off from Jeremy. I need this.

"Tonight?" I ask.

"Absolutely," he replies. His lips trail down my neck and he sucks hard. I'm about to spin around and tell him to forget dinner and spend the next three hours pounding me into oblivion right on his counter tops.

But a group of Heather's guys burst into the kitchen just then. We jump apart.

"What the fuck, man?" Peter Brown and the twins storm in, all frowns. "You made a vagina cake for the other dudes and didn't tell us?"

Kenneth shrugs. "They asked."

"Dude, now they're ahead. We need like, tit pies or twat waffles or something."

"Yeah," Rubin or Reval contributes. "They formed this alliance to try to win the harem. Fuck them. We will not take that lying down." The Russian accent adds just a hint of danger to their outrage.

I bite my lip and raise my brows at Kenneth. "You got this, or you need help?"

He does not look concerned at all by this pissing-contest attitude. "I've got this."

"Okay, then. I'm going to go." I bite my lip and grin. "See you later. Good luck with tit pie."

He scoffs. "Easy. I'll just make them Paris-Brest."

"Sweet," Peter claps his hands and rubs them together. "French tits?"

Kenneth grins. "It's a choux pastry filled with hazelnut and almond cream. The cream would be particularly delicious if you spread it across her—"

"Whoa!" I cut him off and back away. "Heather's friend here. I don't need to hear that part of the recipe."

Instead of letting me just walk away, Kenneth wraps an arm around my shoulders and says innocently, "I'm just going to help them cream her puff."

Behind him, the guys high five.

Kenneth gives them a head nod. "Just a minute."

He escorts me to the door and kisses me on the nose. "Lean in. I want to tell you a secret."

I lean closer and his lips brush my ear as he whispers, "I'm going to think about you every time I make these fuckers a naughty dessert. And the next time you're in my kitchen, all of you is on *my menu*. And my menus take hours to finish." He grins, leans away from me, and nudges me slightly into the hall.

My mind just explodes. My lust-ometer is in the red zone. My panties are swimming. I stumble away from the kitchen thinking 'thank fuck he doesn't do relationships.' Cause that line right there? That woulda' brought me to my knees with a ring if I was that kinda' girl. Damn. There is another kind of ring I like, though. A cock ring. I didn't pack one, but I'm sure there's one in the million boxes of sex crap Heather ordered.

I go back to my villa and search, intending to ravage Kenneth in ways he's never imagined.

Unfortunately, I don't get the chance. The cuntcake incident sets off a number of alliances. Every single one of them demands multiple baked goods from Kenneth. So, my poor, dripping cunt has to take a backseat to the frothing lovepit that Heather's villa becomes over the next three days as every damn alliance strives to compete in the sex war. There are serenades, horrid ear-withering

poems, and even a trek through the tropical forest to
gather flowers.

Unfortunately, tropical flowers come with tropical
spiders. Which come with tropical spider bites. Which
cause Gilbert Perez (secretly nicknamed 'One Up' for his
braggart tendencies) to knock on my door one night, just
as I'm about to say, 'fuck it' and stroll down to Kenneth's
villa in nothing more than a silk robe.

I pull the robe around me and yank the door open to find
—not a sexy chef—but One Up, holding up his right
hand, which is swollen like a misshapen balloon. The
skin looks almost glossy in the moonlight.

"What the fuck! None of the other guys got this shit!"
One Up complains as his lip turns as fat as a garden
hose.

I simply shrug and sigh. "Let me guess. You went off the
path?"

"The best flowers were off the path. I wasn't gonna give
her the same shit as those other dickheads."

I lead Gilbert One Up to a seat in my sea of boxes. I toss
him a container of allergy meds from my medical emergency box and then go to my room and get dressed. I call
our resident surgeon, Andrew.

Unfortunately, I think I might interrupt some private
time he's having with Heather because I'm pretty sure I
hear her voice in the background.

Luckily, Andrew's a decent guy and not a stingy, braggy fuck like the whiner seated on my couch.

Andrew looks Gilbert Perez over but declares there's nothing that can be done here without proper medical equipment. I have the fun job of accompanying Mr. Perez on a boat to the hospital two islands away. The ass takes too many allergy meds and keeps falling asleep on me. I text Heather I want a raise multiple times to no response. Of course.

Finally, I get One Up settled in with a doctor. I get to sign a gigantic hospital bill to have him pumped full of anti-venom and shipped back to the U.S.

So, another potential harem member bites the dust. I'm not too sad as I take a boat back to our island near dawn, however. One Up was hanging by a thread anyway. Only his dick size had gotten him this far, according to Heather, who'd taken numerous photos and notes on Naked Friendship night.

I lean against the side of the speedboat and let the spray smack me in the face. I'm tired and horny as fuck.

Stupid men. And their stupid competitions. Stupid romantic flower-gathering gestures. They have no idea what cuntblocks they are.

The competitive sex war only ends when Heather declares a stalemate after day three. She only stops it after she secretly tells me, "I can't walk. I'm pretty sure my lady bits have been licked clean off."

That makes one of us.

CHAPTER FOURTEEN

Group dates resume. And the next few days have me so busy that even once Kenneth is free, there's hardly time to breathe because my instructions are to allow maximum hoo-ha recovery. This means I have to wear the guys out.

I yank Danny's ass out of bed each morning before dawn so the guys can wake up to a daily round robin tennis tournament. Golf is way too tame. Plus, it gives the three little alliances way too much time to try and plan ahead. Peter Brown's a damn schemer. I guess when you're an ass man, you've always gotta be looking for ways to sneak in the back door.

The one hope I hold onto (after the sex debacle earns several guys their first strikes for a lack of oral skills) is that it seems Andrew, my favorite, is regularly checking in on Heather and bringing her coffee in the morning. I pat myself on the back briefly when I hear that, but then have to yank my arm back off and run a roadblock to keep the twins away from Heather. I end up telling the guys that Heather's making some cut decisions and needs time alone to think about it.

That ratchets up the tension but buys me some time. And it improves their behavior on the next couple group dates. Groping turns into joking, and innuendo turns into … well, no, that stays. They are guys after all.

The beach volleyball group date is a hit. The guys love smacking the ball at one another's faces. Plus, I think the guys get enough sand in their asses that the chafing sends everyone home early that night.

The night is the best. Peace and quiet, my true loves— especially since this crazy-ass scheme of Heather's made me into a 24/7 entertainment director—are present that night.

I slip into a flirty peach dress and go out in search of Kenneth only to find out Alec's flown him to a bigger island so he can restock the pantry. Dammit!

The food bill for ten guys is fucking ridiculous. Especially when I make them do tennis in the morning and the guys not on the group date have to take surfing lessons in the afternoons.

Tim Wu, a relatively quiet guy who never speaks to me, turns out to be a kick ass surfer. The rest spend more time wiping out than anything. But still, it wears them out. Men and toddlers aren't so different. They just grow up to like bigger toys. They guys whine a bit about all the exercise, Matt Rooney had a desk job, so he definitely struggles to keep up with the others. But, I'm here on Heather's orders. And she's happy. She doesn't report any unwanted midnight visitors. So... I'm doing my job.

The group snorkeling date goes off without a hitch, which surprises me. (I keep the paramedics two islands over on speed dial in case of a jelly fish or other random incident). But, as soon as I pat myself on the back, the group horseback riding date takes a turn for the worse. At least for me.

We have to fly to a nearby island for the horses, which are owned by a local tourist joint. That sucks for me because Heather insists I go to take pictures and then she insists that I go on the first round, with her and a majority of the guys.

"Why can't I go on the second flight? There'll be a seat for me."

Heather's eyes narrow. "I'm going on both flights to be able to talk to everyone."

"So?"

"So ... I have plans for the second flight."

"Plans? What the fuck?"

She leans in and whispers. "I'm gonna join the mile-high club."

Dammit all to hell. I stomp over to the plane for the first flight. There are only six seats in the jet's main cabin, and since Heather insists on riding both times there's no damned cabin seat left for me.

The only chair left is in the cockpit. With the asshole captain.

"Hey," Alec says awkwardly as I sit down with a huge camera on my lap.

I ignore him and open the camera's manual. Heather ordered this hulking thing because she wants to look like she's in a magazine. I told her then she probably better hire someone qualified to shoot it. But she just gave me *the look*.

I sigh as I read about focus and shutter speed and then focus again. Because I can't focus. Not with Alec there next to me, breathing and shit. He's like a human magnet. Damn him.

Somehow, I resist the pull to caress his massive biceps as he moves around, flipping buttons, and flicking switches, and turning everything his fingers touch into a dirty sexual metaphor in my mind. I'm so mad at him, though. I have to shift at least four times in my seat because my lady parts want to overlook his assholeness and proposition him again. I have to remind my cooter that we're a package deal and my brain is not up for rejection again. But my cooter puts up a steady protest, like she's doing a sit in and chanting down there. After a while it feels like she might be playing drums, because my hoo-ha is pulsing with need.

I grip the camera manual tighter, lowering my face into it so Alec can't see how hot and bothered I am. Stupid body. Stupid tropical heat wave.

"You're a good woman," Alec says, once we're midair and he's relatively sure we won't crash. "But, I'm not a good guy."

Fuck him for bringing it up! I seethe. As if I needed to hear that! I don't respond. I just stare out the window, admiring the islands and wishing we could land already. Fucking uncomfortable. Uncomfortable enough that my cooter abandons her post at the sit in and starts shaking her head. Even she doesn't want to hear that.

My silence isn't enough of a social cue for Alec. He says, "It just wouldn't have worked out. I didn't want you to get hurt."

Something in me snaps. Instead of just being uncomfortable, I'm pissed. I fucking hate the whole, 'it's me not you' bullshit. I hate the whole assumption that I'm some kind of clinger. How fucking arrogant of him to think that! And say it! I grit out, "It was sex. Not a date. Not a marriage proposal. And you said no. You're allowed to say no. Just like I'm allowed to question your erectile function after you say no."

"What? I'm trying to be nice here," he frowns, which just

makes his damned jawline that much more masculine and lickable.

"Well, you're failing."

"You don't have to be a bitch about it. I'm just not the right kind of guy for you. I don't do relation—"

I throw my head back in a bitter laugh, cutting him off. Then I shake my head slightly as I stare into his deep brown eyes. "You're an idiot."

He just bites his lip and turns away from me. But I'm not done. Oh no. You want to open this can of worms? Prepare to be on the hook for the fallout. I lean forward over my armrest and ignore how the camera jabs me in the stomach. I whisper-shout, "I'm sick of men thinking I want a damned relationship. What the fuck is it about me? Do I need to get a nose piercing and some tattoos in order to be independent and wild enough for you? Fuck that shit."

"Whoa, you're blowing this way out of proportion."

"No. I'm not. All I wanted was sex. I don't want marriage. I don't want babies. Not from you—or anyone. But, especially not from you. So, just shut up and fly the plane." I end on a low note and lean back in my seat. I immediately start kicking myself. I totally should have stopped talking after the word 'anyone.' My voice got all weak and emotional during that last bit. Fuck. Now, he probably thinks I'm a whiner. But I doubt it will get better if I say anything else. I'm kind of proud of myself for saying anything at all. I mean, normally, I hate confrontation. But he was making me uncomfortable anyway. And I was drowning in awkward lust. Maybe it was a lust bomb. Maybe that's why I exploded. Just too much pressure and *bam*!

We finish the flight without saying another word. His jaw is tight the entire way. I can't help glancing over at him, even as I fiddle with the camera, pretending I'm gonna be able to figure this contraption out. I 'accidentally' take a few photos of him.

"What are you doing?"

"Just getting fodder for my dart board." It seems, now that I've unleashed the beast, it's a lot easier to be confrontational with him. Hmmm… I'll need to remember that.

He doesn't respond because he has to land. And I'm stupidly giddy over getting the last word. Heather never lets me have the last word. Neither does my mother.

The second the plane stops, I'm out of my seat. But Alec hops up as well and smacks into me, making me fall back down into my chair.

He leans down, eyes glittering with fury. "Oops." His hand reaches forward and touches the camera strap around my neck. The huge ass camera is hanging down off my side since I fell. Alec sticks his finger under the strap and slowly drags his digit down. Doing so makes the camera lift and settle onto my lap. It also lets Alec's index finger trace down over my breast. He lingers over my nipple.

My breath catches.

That's when the asshole smiles, straightens, and walks away.

Fuck. Even when he's angry as hell and being a jerk, he's hotter than the devil's balls.

What the hell? That shouldn't be possible.

I spend the entire time on the drive to the stables just fuming.

My mood doesn't get better when Heather arrives with the second group of guys, chatting excitedly with the Asian guy whose name I forgot. All nine remaining guys are coming on this date. She insisted.

I walk over to Heather only to realize Danny's behind her. He was on the flight? I grit my teeth and smile. I don't need a gnat in my eye after I just got done arguing with Alec the asshole. It's piling insult onto injury. But it's done.

Danny walks over, slings an arm across my shoulders like we're old friends and says, "Heard about your argument with Alec."

"How?"

"Pretty sure the whole plane heard you tell him off."

I facepalm. Damn professional, Katie, I scold myself. Way to be.

Danny's hand squeezes my shoulder. As if him touching me is comforting. It's not. It's just a reminder that I'm horny as fuck and Kenneth and I haven't gotten to make bacon together. We haven't had time for him to mash my potatoes, make the cheese. There's been no chance for him to chop my block. My mind has had way too much time to picture us in his kitchen in way too many positions and come up with way too many metaphors for how I want him to suck on my sour citrus... even thinking about it gets me riled up.

"I told Alec we're dating," Danny says, matter-of-fact.

My sexy thoughts collapse. My head whips up to look at him and I shove his arm off me. "That's a lie."

"It doesn't have to be."

"I don't date. I have fuck buddies." Might as well lay that out there, since apparently, I give off some 'dating-type' vibe to men.

Danny's jaw drops. But he doesn't look disgusted. He looks delighted. "Oh my God. Can you say that into my phone?" Danny pulls his phone out of his pocket and opens an app. He holds it up toward me. "Please. Pretty please."

"I don't date. I have fuck buddies."

"I'm totally jerking off to that later. Gonna be my ringtone."

"Gross!" I say, but I can't help but be a little amused by him. And a tiny little piece of me tosses her hair and presses her boobs together, like, 'Fuck yeah! A guy that hot is jerking off to thoughts of me.'

Danny smiles and holds up a finger. "Ah, but you didn't say lie."

"I believe you'll jerk off. I'm pretty sure that's a daily thing for you."

"Sadly, yes. But it could be a daily thing for you instead." He leans forward and licks his lips in a salacious manner.

"That is so tempting."

He laughs, "Lie!"

I shrug. "Sorry. Got an arrangement with the chef. If only I can get a free minute."

Danny winks. "Well—if you ever want a quickie, I'm a one-minute man—"

Like that, Danny's humor bursts through the clouds hanging over my head. My laugh travels all the way to my belly. I have to hold onto his shoulders to keep from toppling over.

"You're supposed to call me on the lie," Danny says.

"What if I don't think it is one?" I pant, swiping at tears.

"Then you just lost five grand," he shrugs.

I narrow my eyes. "You'd have to prove it wasn't a lie."

Danny leans down and his blue eyes hint at the naughty thoughts he has. His finger reaches out and traces my lips. "Happy to prove it. Anytime."

CHAPTER FIFTEEN

Anthony Drake, the blondie, ends up getting death's horse on the horseback riding date. The horse's head is hanging almost to the fucking ground. He wheezes and coughs every few seconds.

I argue with the tour guide about providing us with a sick horse. He simply says, "It's just allergies. He's fine."

"Swap him out."

"Your group is so big; it's taking all our horses today. I don't have another."

The front of the group has already started down the trail with another guide.

I climb off my own horse and swap Anthony. The poor horse could at least use a break carrying a lighter passenger. But as we head down the trail, I fall farther and farther behind.

"Guys!" I call out when my horse stops for its fifth break. It wheezes. I call out again, because everyone else is too busy ogling the scenery or looking down the cliff at the ocean on our right side, or into the tropical forest at a troop of monkeys that are plucking at fruit that's been strategically placed in the trees so that tourists can get their 'exotic animal experience.' I'm too busy with my farm animal experience to enjoy the exotic animals.

I end up sliding off my horse and walking next to him, because it's fucking faster that way. I yank him along. Apparently, I yank a little hard and this makes him rear up and bray.

That scares the shit out of the monkeys and a mother-fucking ton of green mangos get thrown at my head. I scream, and dodge, and run into the trees like I'm in some balls-to-the-wall action movie. My heart certainly feels like it is. A mango smacks me in the neck. Another smashes the side of my head.

Fuck! I feel like I got beaned by a softball. I put a hand to my neck. Suddenly, I'm woozy. Black spots flitter through my field of vision.

I see a horse coming back down the path. That's when I realize that I'm not on the path anymore. And death's horse is nowhere to be found. BJ Thomas—the New Yorker—sets his horse to a trot.

"BJ!" I call out. He doesn't answer.

I try again. "BJ! Help me!" His eyes flicker briefly over

the trees, but then he speeds up and disappears around a bend. Fuck.

I stumble toward the path, but I'm feeling dizzy. Shit. I hope BJ had to take a shit and he'll turn around and be back...

I hear another set of hooves. Danny's horse trots around the corner.

"DANNY!" I scream like I'm out of my mind.

He stops the horse. So, I feel justified. And a little bit like puking.

"Danny," this time my voice comes out as more of a moan.

Danny dismounts and stomps through the brush. He finds me clinging to a tree. He doesn't even ask what's wrong. He just scoops me into his arms.

He grabs his horse's reins and starts walking back toward the stables where we started. "What the hell happened?"

"You're ruining your rescue," I croak.

"How can you ruin a rescue?"

"By talking... and not sweeping me up onto the horse."

"I'm pretty sure we'd both fall off if I tried that."

I shrug a shoulder but stop because it makes my neck hurt. "Fine. Be a mediocre hero. Whatever."

That makes Danny's entire body stiffen. "I. Am. Not. Mediocre." He drops the reins and stomps to the side of the horse, throwing me up onto the grey beast so hard I almost slide over the other side. Then he smashes his foot into a stirrup and lifts his leg to mount—and the horse moves. It takes a step forward, causing Danny to fall backward, legs and arms flailing like a cartoon character until he lands right onto his ass.

I burst into laughter.

"Fuck! That's not funny," he grouses. Danny climbs to his feet, rubbing his ass. He walks to the front of the horse, snatches the reins, and yanks forward so that the beast and I both jolt a bit.

"Hey, that hurts my neck."

"Well, you deserve it for laughing," he narrows his eyes at me.]

"How'd you get hurt again?"

"The monkeys attacked me."

He doubles over in laughter. "Animals have good instincts, I guess."

"You mean like the horse not letting you ride him?"

He flips me the bird.

I stick out my tongue then grin. I'm enjoying this side of him. Picking on him. Having him pick back. It's kind of like we're friends. It's what Heather and I do.

I suddenly feel vulnerable. Like somehow, that revelation means something. Nervous bubbly energy bounces around in my stomach and I don't know why. Who cares if we're friends? I've been friends with a guy before. But I realize ... I kind of haven't. I haven't really let a guy be my friend since Michael. Since I was twenty-one years old.

"What the hell's that face?" Danny asks as he yanks the reins of his unwilling horse again to force it into a walk.

"That horse is gonna bite you."

"Horses don't bite," Danny scoffs.

"Fine. They don't." Let him find out for his arrogant self.

"You're avoiding the question," Danny needles. "What the hell was that face? Is there something on my ass?" He twists, trying to look, but the horse is moving so he has to keep walking.

I glance down at his sports shorts, which do absolutely zero to hide the fact that his ass is like sculpted marble. Each step shows it flexing and relaxing. I realize what a fantastic view I have. Fuck the ocean. The undulation of the waves ain't got nothing on Danny's ass. I swallow. I realize what the nervous feeling in my stomach is.

I look up to meet Danny's knowing grin; he's turned and is watching me over his shoulder. That grin says, 'I caught you.' So does the wink that follows.

"You're gonna walk into a tree that way," I tell him.

"No, I won't."

"Happened to me at Disneyland when I was a kid," I tell him. "Got distracted looking at a character and *wham*! Tree jumped out of nowhere."

"You still haven't answered my question," Danny presses but does turn and briefly look at the path in front of him before turning his bright blue eyes back to me.

His eyes rake over me, causing the swirling nervous energy to overtake the headache pounding in my head. My emotions dance like ... like a toddler that needs to pee. Awkwardly. Reluctantly. I'm a toddler who wants to deny reality because she wants to keep playing play-dough, dammit. I just want to keep doing what I'm doing and not have to think about unpleasant things. Like toilet bowls or rejection.

How the hell can I have a crush on Danny? Not fucking possible. Nope. No. Especially not when I'm supposed to have an arrangement with Kenneth. Nope. This is not attraction. It's just I'm not used to having male friends anymore. That's what this is. That's all.

I glance at him and find I can't hold eye contact. Fuck! But he's waiting and I have to say something. I twist my hands nervously over the saddle's pommel as I squeak out, "I just realized that we're ... friends."

Danny doesn't say anything as he leads me up over the final hill before the stables. He leads me all the way to the barn. I swing my feet over to one side of the horse so I can jump down. But Danny stops me. He puts his hands on my hips and lifts me off. He pulls me into his chest and slides my body slowly down his.

My breath catches. My nipples pebble. That nervous energy inside me whips itself up into a cyclone. Danny leans into me, his hands brushing up along my waist.

"I'm not the only one who's a liar," he whispers.

Then he grins and walks off, whistling, while I stand next to the stable with a swollen head, a swollen heart, and a very soaked fucking thong.

CHAPTER SIXTEEN

I avoid Danny and Alec on the plane ride back to the island by hiding in the bathroom the entire flight. I don't care if the entire world thinks I'm shitting myself. I cannot deal with the stomach-roiling mess I turn into when I stand next to either one.

I'm still pissed at Alec. And Danny's long stares ever since he called me a liar make my knees tremble. I can't deal with that shit. Any of it. I'm here on business. I'm here for Heather. They are distractions from what I'm really here to do. Work. Build a business and a life for myself. Something bigger and braver than I would have had if Heather had never won the lotto. Something better than Doc Strife's office or mom's critique-filled family dinners. Those men are nothing but emotional vipers, out to poison me. I don't have time for that. I'll stick with Kenneth and his offer of no-strings sex. That's all I've ever needed anyway, I think as I brace my arms against the bathroom walls during our descent.

Heather knocks on the bathroom door and asks, "You okay?"

I just yell, "Puking!"

I wait until we've landed and taxied to a stop to exit the bathroom. Then I force my way between Jeremiah Bible and Andrew so that I can exit in peace. I ignore Danny trying to get closer to me and speed walk down the tarmac.

I just need to fuck Kenneth. Then, all these stupid feelings and anger over an insult that doesn't really matter will go away. It's all just hormonal bullshit anyway, I tell myself.

I hit the trees and the path to the villas. I'm about to shed my shoes and book it toward the kitchen but Heather's hand on my arm stops me.

I turn to face her, and she looks serious. She leans in and whispers, "I need to make another cut."

I fake smile at the guys and pull Heather down the side path to her villa. "Thanks, guys for the excellent group date! There's parasailing available later this afternoon for those of you who want to go, and I've got something special planned for dinner!" I make sure to put myself between them and Heather and wave like a happy maniac so no one can try to talk her into an individual date.

I follow her to her villa and steal some headache medicine from her bathroom. She paces her bedroom, alternating between playing with the gauzy canopy and wringing her hands.

"I want to cut Tim Wu," she tells me. But, unlike normal Heather, she sounds a bit nervous.

"Did he do something? What's wrong?"

She rubs her brows, circling like she has a headache. "I think he's gay."

"What?"

"I think ... I think he just signed up for this as a way to meet other guys."

I see red. I'm pissed. Did I miss something in my evals? Dammit! I probably did. I've hardly paid attention to Tim since he arrived. He's a hot Asian guy, but kind of quiet. He never shocked me like Peter Brown or felt overly aggressive like One Up.

Fuck, I didn't even give the guy a nickname in my head to sort him from the others. That's how little I've paid attention to Tim Wu. I go over to Heather's dresser and pull open the drawer where I initially put the guy's files so she could review them in her spare time. I yank them out, saying, "This is my fault. I'm sorry—"

"No!" Heather grabs my hand. "It's not like you could have screened for this! And ... I feel guilty asking him to leave. Because ... honestly, I think he and Matt have a connection."

I pull up Tim's file and Matt's and glare at their photos. I'm really pissed I didn't notice this. But then, maybe, if today hadn't gone so wonky, I would have. "Want me to cut both?"

"No ... I mean, they're both sweet! And kind. And Matt, he and I have a little connection. But I don't feel *anything* with Tim. Super awkward. But, should it all be about me with this harem thing? I mean ... should the guys only be into me?"

"I thought that was the point of a harem." It's the fucking point in all my books.

"You're supposed to be the center. Like Emelle."

"You made me the ditzy character, didn't you?" Heather scowls. "You always make me the ditzy one. You bitch!"

I hold up my hands to pacify her. "She's the only main RH character with hair half as good as yours. But you're missing the point. You know, Emelle's the one that helps the genfins bond and see through their dumb guy feud and stuff. She helps them be better people."

Heather sighs. "Yeah. Maybe ... I don't know! It just seems ... not fair. I mean, I'm keeping the twins. But, seriously, I think they're bi. And the sex with them ..." She fans herself. "But I think it's unfair to keep Tim around when I'm not even into him." She growls and throws herself on the bed. "This was supposed to be easy and fun!"

I set down the files and move closer to her. If she's not having fun, then I'm totally failing at this job. If she's not having fun, I'm failing as a friend, too.

"It hasn't been fun?" I ask nervously. "Not even snorkeling when you saw the sea turtle?"

She gives a little grin. "Okay, that was fun."

"Or when you got naughty desserts for days?"

She rolls her eyes. "And that."

"Or when the guys came up with that rap, sat you in a chair, surrounded you so they could sing, and ended up spitting all over you with their beatboxing?"

She narrows her eyes at me.

"What? *I* thought that was fun." Andrew and the twins had paired up for that, changing alliances for the night to create ... the worst rap in the world. So, so bad. So hilarious. I swipe tears away at the memory. Then I imitate the guys and repeat my favorite verse, which I made them perform multiple times until I had it memorized. "Some fellas go for the triple crown,

Three holes in one, they're turkey bound.

Some guys bounce a girl like *ping pong*,

Gonna rama lam her with their *ding dong*!

Who's at the back door?

Peter Brown is back for more!

But our lady shoves him aside,

She wants to rev her engine and go for ride.

She knows just what to do.

We'll work her over 'til our lips be blue.

She'll drive us like a cat outta hell,

Stick shift's her jam, she knows it well. Holla!"

I even add my own beat box. I collapse into a chair, laughing until my ribs hurt. I swipe at another tear or two. "They really outdid themselves with that one. Gah. I mean, the slam on Peter and everything. And Russian rapping ..." I put my hand to my heart. "That's gonna be your anthem for life now, you know that right? When we're old and in retirement homes, I'm totally making you an embroidered pillow that says 'Stick Shift's Her Jam.'"

Heather laughs and throws a pillow at me. "Shut up. They tried. Which is more than most guys do. They're so sweet. All of them." She grows pensive again. "I mean ... I didn't think this would be hard."

I shrug. "Sorry. I guess ... life is complicated when you like multiple guys." I know mine is.

"Fuck. Don't be wise right now. Just get me alcohol."

"Yes, ma'am!" I salute and raid the minibar in her fridge. "Tiny bottles of wine?"

"Midget wine!" she squeals.

"Pretty sure it's dwarf wine."

"Fairy wine."

"Imp wine."

"Gnome wine."

"Shit—I'm outta little magical creatures," Heather admits.

"Pixies, leprachauns, brownies."

"Show off. Now I want a brownie."

"Me too."

We clink mini bottles and I unscrew the lid to the white wine. I down half of it with a sip. Heather takes hers like a shot, then opens another.

I clear my throat and say, "I'll tell Tim he can pack his things and have him on the plane before dinner. I just have to check on how many flight hours we have left with Alec. I'm going to have to re-up soon. Anything else?"

"Yes. What's up with you and Danny? He's totally been making doe-eyes at you." Heather waggles her brows.

My face heats. "He was not."

She laughs. "Your face says otherwise. Was I right? I *knew* I saw the spark between you guys. I was r-i-i-ght."

"He's a liar!"

She shrugs. "So are you. But you're calling him on it, right? Wouldn't want to have to dock your pay."

"Yes, I'm calling him on it," I grumble as I down the second half of my wine.

"Fine, you don't want to talk about him, then tell me about the pilot," Heather demands, sitting up at the head of the bed.

I whirl around to look at her.

"I'm not totally oblivious, you know!" she smirks. "I think you could have a really fun threesome."

"I'm not sleeping with either of them."

"Why the fuck not? They're hot."

"I have an arrangement with the chef," I sniff.

Her eyes widen. "What the hell?" She laughs and drinks a third wine cooler. She shakes her head. "You've got your own damn harem going."

"I do not!"

She stares at me with disbelief. "Um. Yeah. You totally do."

I cross my arms. "Not true." I don't tell her how Alec

rejected me. Because a little part of me is still hurt about that. Even though a bigger part of me is mad at the stupid-ass assumptions he made about me. "I told you I have an arrangement with Kenneth."

"Oh, Kenneth. He made all those naughty desserts? He'd totally be down for sharing. Let me tell you, having one guy eat you out while another sucks on your—"

"NO!" I cover my ears and shoot out of my seat. "I don't want the details."

"Since when?"

"Since I've got to look each of these guys in the eyes in a couple hours. It's different if I only see the guy every couple months. The embarrassing details fade."

She shakes her head. "Yeah. Shane Paul was a shit husband. Always gone."

I go over to her and wrap an arm around her shoulders. "Hey, you kicked him to the curb, won the lotto, have tons of hot guys here just dying to be with you—I'd say you're pretty much beating him at life."

She gives me a smug smile. "I am, aren't I?"

I shrug. "Well, you've always had him beat in the friend department. But, now ... I mean ..."

"Want to know something? Not like super-detailed so you can still look at the guys but like a little detail?" she bites her lip, all excited.

I can't tell her no. "What?"

"I never knew that the orgasms Shane Paul gave me were just, like, 'meh' orgasms. But now, I know what a rolling fucking orgasm feels like. OMG. Never going back!"

I grab two more mini bottles, twist off the tops and raise my bottle. "To guys who know how to properly go downtown!"

"To the poon monsoon!" Heather cheers.

I groan. "Way, way to graphic."

She just laughs.

I take a sip of my new wine but set it down. I've still got shit to do. "Alright. I'm on my way to boot Wu. Anyone else you want to get rid of?" I stop in her doorway.

She squints at me. "Can you do me a favor? Like a weird one?"

"Like the time we swapped bras on that double date because yours didn't push your boobs together enough?"

"Kinda but not really."

I roll my eyes. "Just ask already."

"Would you keep an eye on Tony?"

"Anthony Drake? The real estate guy? With the great white smile?" I cock my head.

"Yeah. We have good chemistry, but I don't quite trust him. But I don't know why."

I shrug. "Go with your gut. You have other guys here. You could boot him."

She bites her lip. "Not ready for that. Tim's hard enough. Can you just maybe ... follow him around a little? See if he's weird or something."

"Sure. Why not?"

My phone buzzes with another calendar reminder. "Alright. I better go. I need to get another embarrassing photos slideshow ready for after dinner."

Heather's jaw drops. "What?" she shrieks.

I giggle as I run out the door. "Kidding!"

Next time I embarrass her, it'll be much worse.

CHAPTER SEVENTEEN

I change from my horseback riding get-up into a bright yellow dress and flip flops. It's too warm and muggy to stay in jeans all evening. Then I deal with Wu. He doesn't look surprised when I tell him Heather's cutting him. But when I tell him he needs to leave, he does look heartbroken.

"Now?"

"Them's the rules," I shrug. "Sorry."

"But can I just—"

I shake my head. "The plane's already running."

Wu packs without another word. He does sneak in a text, but I pretend I don't see, because he gets teary-eyed when he does it.

We reach the plane and Alec opens the door and comes down the stairs. He greets us with a nod. Alec opens his stupid mouth, but I cut him off. "We're down on flight hours, right?"

Alec nods. "Yeah. After I take this guy, I've got someone else who scheduled some hours on this baby with another pilot. They need an emergency flight, so I have to leave the plane a couple islands over for pick up. We won't have a plane for a few days."

I nod. I don't ask where he's staying, even though I'm tempted. "I'll get online and re-up those hours—"

"I'm taking the boat back here tonigh—"

We both stop and awkwardly stare at one another. That annoying humming, high-energy buzz my body gets around him starts up. Dammit all. He's like a stupid zaplight. The damn kind with a blue glow that draw the bugs in. Only he attracts women. A literal lady killer.

I take a step back, trying to get away from the physical effect he has on me.

Alec goes toward the steps of the jet. I turn around to walk back to the villas in the pink light of sunset, only to find Matt Rooney running down the tarmac full-speed, waving one arm wildly.

I guess Heather was right. Matt and Tim did form a connection. Apparently, a strong one. As Matt gets closer, I realize he's got a suitcase under one arm. So, he's not just running up to say goodbye.

"I think you might have a second passenger," I turn and tell Alec.

Matt rushes up to us. His black hair is windblown and he's winded, but he gives us a smile as he asks, "Room for one more?"

I nod. "Of course."

"Tell Heather I really appreciate everything. Everything. But ..."

I smile and nod up at the plane. "She'll be thrilled you two found each other here. Go get your man."

Matt bolts up the stairs. I hear a wail from the plane. It sounds like a romantic movie reunion. The kind that make me cry. As it is, I get tears in my eyes.

Alec, on the other hand, gets a stern face. "No sex on the plane, you two!" he barks as he marches up the stairs. "Just kidding. Put down a blanket so I don't have to bleach the whole thing. You wouldn't believe how hard cum shots are to get out of this upholstery."

Alec smiles at me before he pulls the plane door shut.

I forgive him a little just then. He's not a completely bad guy. Just bad for me. For whatever reason...

I watch Matt and Tim fly off into the sunset and I feel a little ping of regret. Michael never would have run down a tarmac after me. And now, no one will. Damn. I shove that self-pity aside. Stupid hormones. Stupid female mating instincts. That's all this is. Well, I'll solve that problem.

I yank my phone out of my pocket and dial the kitchen. Predictably, Kenneth doesn't answer. It goes to voicemail, just like every other time I called his kitchen before the trip. Fuck it. I'll just show up and rip off my clothes. I'm done waiting for the right time.

I yank open the kitchen door to find Kenneth sitting at a worktable, hunched over what looks like a dress. What the hell?

I step inside and can't help asking, "Are you ... sewing?"

"Yes," Kenneth's face is screwed up in concentration.

"I need sex," I tell him. Might as well be direct.

He grins but doesn't look up. "I'm almost finished. Five minutes?"

I nod and sit near him on a stepstool. "What is that?" I lean forward to look at his work. At first, I thought he was repairing his chef coat or something. But, he's not. He's carefully pulling thin slices of eggplant and sewing them together. "What kind of recipe is that?"

"It's called edible clothing."

"Oh. Um. Okay. What's it for?"

"Dinner," he leans forward and tightens a stich before moving onto the next strip of eggplant.

"Wait. What?"

Kenneth straightens and holds up what looks like a flowy, short miniskirt. It's white with the red seeds and the purple skin of the eggplant creating a playful pattern. The slices of eggplant are layered to create ruffles. It's actually really fucking cute. I'd consider buying it if it weren't made of food. But what the hell is with food clothing?

My face must show Kenneth what I'm thinking, because he explains, "Heather requested a sensual dinner tonight. Something that would get the men riled up. So ... after much consideration, I've decided *she's* on the menu. Veggie skirt. Bacon bra. I used the new pineapple passionfruit flavoring from your hard candies and made some edible underwear. And ..." he holds up a mini zucchini. "All natural, all edible butt plug."

I cringe and turn away. "I don't think that's— "

"I set my own menu!" Kenneth's voice smacks down my protest as he lovingly sets the mini skirt down. "Heather's already been summoned. She'll be here in a few minutes. I'll help her get ready. And then ..." his eyes glitter. "Then you're mine."

I sink back on my stool. "I don't know if I'm in the mood anymore after hearing about edible butt plugs."

He laughs. "Ah, pretty girl. I made some special things just for you."

"Butt plugs?" I widen my eyes and clench the sides of my seat. I'm half-joking, half-not. If he pulls out another zucchini, I'm booking it.

"No, beautiful. Just jewelry."

"Oh." Jewelry I can handle. I think.

Kenneth goes over to another worktable. He picks up a short string of red beads and walks toward me. His eyes lock onto mine and don't let go.

My breath starts coming faster just at the look in his eyes. So intent on me. So focused. He stops just in front of me, his thighs touching my knees. Even that little touch sends waves of lust spiraling through me. My stomach tightens in anticipation. My mouth dries out. There's a primal connection between us. Slowly, very slowly, he takes my right hand in both of his. He puts the red bracelet on my skin. It's cold, almost wet-cold, to the touch.

"What is it?" I breathe.

He doesn't answer, just lifts my hand close to his face so he can see to knot the tiny fishing line of the bracelet. Then his eyes go back to mine. He pulls my wrist up to his lips and kisses it. He keeps my hand at his mouth and his eyes search mine. Then his tongue snakes out and traces my pulse.

My heart speeds up. My thoughts get hazy. I've never been seduced by someone like this before. He's so slow.

Methodical, measuring my reaction every step of
the way.

I watch as his eyes drop to see where my nipples have
pebbled, as if he knew that's what would happen when
he licked me there. I didn't even know that would
happen. The wrist is a hot zone? But, every part of my
body thrums in awareness as he traces kisses across my
palm, all while maintaining eye contact.

My nipples grow as hard as glass and I didn't wear a bra
underneath this dress. I know they're straining against
the cotton. I know he can see their peaks pressing out,
begging for attention. But he doesn't move toward them.
No matter how much I want him to—no, Kenneth stays
focused on my wrist.

His teeth scrape the inside, right near my pulse. And that
makes me feel vulnerable on a primal level. Which just
makes me want to surrender to him all the more. He
sucks my skin into his mouth and releases it. And then his
lips trace a soft pattern down my wrist, wrapping around
one of red beads. He crushes it in his teeth and a streak as
red as blood runs down the inside of my arm.

Kenneth points his tongue and lazily traces the red drops,
pulling me off the stool and urging my body closer to his.

"Pomegranete seeds," he whispers.

I can feel the heat of him now. And in my flip flops he's
taller than me in just the right ways. If I went on my
tiptoes, I could kiss him. If I bent forward and unzipped

his pants, I could take him in my mouth. I feel his erection prod at my stomach and my free hand goes to stroke it.

Kenneth stops me.

"No, darling. Take off your dress."

I back up and whip my dress over my head. My hair gets a little stuck, (a far cry from a porno undressing), but Kenneth helps me untangle myself without laughing ... so at least he's not a jerk about it. Instead, he maintains that calm, intense sensual energy the entire time.

He stares down at my breasts once they're free. His finger comes up and traces the tan line on my chest, the triangles made by my bikinis. His finger slides up and down to where my creamy skin begins. His touch is light, it tickles like a feather and my knees go weak. He licks his lips and I try to tempt him into licking my breasts the way he just licked my wrist. I use my left hand to cup my left breast and point the brick-red nipple at him enticingly. He inhales sharply, drops his finger from my breasts, and strides quickly back to his worktable.

"What did I do wrong—"

He's turning and striding back toward me before I can say his name. He has a bright yellow necklace in his hands, and he tosses it around my neck before I realize what's happening. It bounces against my skin with a wet splash and then settles. It's long. The beads fall below my

breasts. I can smell the fruit immediately. "Pineapple?"
I ask.

Kenneth doesn't answer. He's too busy sweeping back my
brown hair and licking at beads on my neck. He crushes a
bit of pineapple and repeats his earlier torture. His
tongue laves my collarbone, lapping up the fragrant juice.
His head moves down between my breasts, his hair tick-
ling them. His tongue traces the middle bead that lies just
above my naval.

I take his hair in my hands, ready to shove his head lower.
But he gently pries my hands away from his brown locks
and puts them down by my side. Then he uses his teeth
to grab the very bottom pineapple bead; his mouth pulls
the necklace up, away from my body and shifts it over,
moving the necklace until it settles right on top of my
nipple. The cold from the pineapple instantly makes my
nipple incredibly sensitive.

I gasp. I can't help it. My head curves back. Oh my
fucking God. I love this.

I love it even more when Kenneth's warm breath blows
on my nipple. The cold pineapple blocks him at the
center but the heat and cold on my sensitive skin makes
my toes curl. Fucking hell. I could almost come like this.
My breasts start to heave as my breathing speeds up.

And that's when Kenneth swoops in. His teeth clench
around the pineapple on my nipple. He bites down on it,
biting my nipple in the process.

Lightning bolts of lust shoot through me. "Fuck!" I pant.

Kenneth's teeth release my nipple just as the pain gets to be a bit too much. He bites off that piece of pineapple, straightens and watches my eyes as he eats it.

Shit, just watching him eat has my pussy fluttering in anticipation. My hands reach for him again, but he places them back by my sides and then dives back to my belly. He grabs the necklace with his teeth once more and moves the pineapple beads over so that it hangs between my breasts, so that no juice drips onto his bite mark. His mouth trails lazily up my chest, not so much kissing as just mouthing me. He traces up my neck, sending shivers down my spine. By the time he gets to my chin, my entire body is on fire with need.

And that's when he kisses me. Rough. Not soft like his tongue has been on my wrist and body. No, his tongue owns mine. His tongue battles with me, beats my mouth into submission. He tastes of pineapple and I know that the fruit has been forever ruined for me. Every time I eat it, I'm going to be reminded of this moment. The moment Kenneth claimed my body.

My lust is so strong, I'm such a whirlwind of need and heat and hormones, that he has to grab my ass to keep me upright. I try to grind into him, but he backs his pelvis away. And then his lips leave mine.

I seek his, whimpering in protest.

He just chuckles. "Oh no, you're not ready yet. It's time for you to simmer."

His eyes—those damned deceiving sweet-guy-next-door eyes—spark as he slides down my body and removes my panties. He has me step out of them and my flip flops. His hand teases up my thigh but stops short of his goal.

"Please," I whisper. "I need it." I'm at his mercy. I'm so crazy wet, and my spine is already tingling with those pre-orgasm shivers. Fuck me. I just need him to fuck me.

He leads me over to a completely clear worktable and I'm so excited my hands are shaking. Yes. Yes!

He helps me hop up onto the table, pulls off the pineapple necklace and tosses it aside. "Lie back."

Kenneth comes around to the back of the table and puts a warm towel under my head, so I'm not resting completely against the hard, polished wood. I smile in thanks and my heartbeat speeds up as he moves back around toward my feet. He bends my legs so that each foot rests on the table top.

"Spread," he commands.

I spread. He grabs my ankles and pulls them further apart. I'm wide open, gaping.

His deep intense eyes move from my face, down my breasts, and settle on my slit. Then his hand reaches up and cups my primed sex. His fingers rest on the very thin trimmed patch of hair there. My entire body tightens in anticipation.

Kenneth leans forward between my legs and his voice is gruff as he whispers, "I'm gonna fuck you in ways you didn't even know you could get fucked."

My pussy flutters at those words. Literally flutters. Like possibly a level one orgasm. Like an earthquake that's there, deep inside, a foreshock warning you that bigger, life-changing, building-toppling moments are coming. His hand presses into me. He knows exactly what he's doing.

"Fuck," I whisper. My eyes close.

Kenneth's hand moves away, and I keep my eyes closed for a second, expecting to hear him tossing his clothes off. I don't hear that.

When my eyelids pop open, I see Kenneth setting a big metallic bowl of steaming corn on the cob next to me. He pulls one cob out of the bowl and slides it down my thigh. The heat and the texture are a new sensation. Hot, wet, tickles. If tickles could be wet. It's ... different. He slides it down the other thigh. I don't think I like it nearly as much as the wrist or my nipple, until Kenneth rolls it right *there*. He slides it up and down the outside of my lips.

The heat is delicious. It's just as hot as a dick. But the texture. The soft little warm nubs trace up and down my inner lips. And it's goddamned-frickin'-tastic. I go as mindless and as dumb as Frankenstein's monster.

"Oh. Ohhhhh," I moan. "Fuck me." What the mother-fuck is going on? My brain starts to ask questions, but I shut that shit down quick. I don't want to ask questions. I just want to feel. Kenneth knows what the fuck he's doing with food.

He slides the cob back and forth in a regular pattern until the heat dissipates. Then he sets that cob aside and grabs a new one from the bowl. The fresh heat sends a wave of pleasure right through me. It courses up my spine and sends my head spinning.

My hands smack down onto the table and my pelvis lifts, seeking that heat, begging Kenneth to put that heat right between my lips. He does just the tip, teasing me before sliding it up and over. He uses other his hand to pull back my hood and the warm, wet heat bumps over my clit. Again and again and again. I melt into a mind-altering orgasm. My hips hump the air and I moan, clawing at the table.

When I come back down, I'm not Katie anymore. I'm some weird, sex-crazed freak. Holy motherfuck, I realize. I like to fuck fruit.

CHAPTER EIGHTEEN

Kenneth uses his hand to help me up from the table. My legs are still a little shaky and my hands are asleep. All the blood has fled elsewhere.

Kenneth turns me around so I'm facing the table. He places my hands on the wood and uses his feet to make me spread.

Yes. He's going to fuck me. I'm so ready. So fucking ready. At this point, after the orgasm he's given me, I don't even care if he wants to shove a zuchinni in my ass. I'm in such a sex haze that I'll do anything. Anything.

Kenneth's arms come around me and I feel the corn on the cob tracing down my belly.

This time, I'm not weirded out. This time there is only anticipation about what mind-blowing thing he's going to do to me next. He presses the cob against my nether region. And holds it there. Then one of his hands reaches up and grabs mine. He wraps my fingers around the corn on the cob.

Then he whispers, "Keep a steady rhythm. You can come three times before I get back. But no more. And nothing better enter that gorgeous pussy before my dick. Not your fingers. Not that cob. You hear me?"

Shit. I nearly come just at those commands. Goddamn.

"Yes," my voice is breathy as he helps me get a rhythm started.

"I'm gonna get Heather ready. Then I'll be back."

"Unh," my response isn't even a word. I'm so close to that next orgasm. Kenneth's hand reaches out and closes over mine. He slows the pace, keeping me on the brink. "Only three," he whispers.

Then he steps away. I hear him gather up his things. The door opens and shuts behind him. And that's the last thing I remember before I set myself off on a rolling orgasm that feels like it lasts for days.

Kenneth takes a while to get Heather dressed. I go through four more corncobs. And I cheat and give myself one extra orgasm.

When Kenneth comes back, I hear him slam the door and walk over to me.

Smack! He spanks my ass hard. "I could hear you from

the dining room. How many orgasms did I say you could have?"

Fuck! I bite my lip, turned on but anxious at the same time. Is he really mad at me? I look over my shoulder to find him unbuttoning his shirt and grinning. "I knew you'd cheat."

His naughty smile makes me giddy. Giddiness turns back into lust when he pulls open his shirt to reveal very cut pecs and a thin set of abdominals. His happy trail looks enticing.

I straighten and reach out, letting my fingers trace down the soft little hairs. I look up at Kenneth as I reach for the button on his pants, my eyes asking if I can undo it.

He nods. I pull the button and then slowly undo the zipper, enjoying the thrill of anticipation and the tiny bit of control I get from making him wait. I leisurely pull his pants down his legs and he steps out of them. I realize he has bare feet. He must have gotten rid of his shoes when he walked in.

My hands reach up for his boxers and I slowly pull those down, admiring the length of his dick. He's definitely bigger than Jeremy. His dick is long and curved slightly. I lean forward and place my mouth around the head. There's already a couple drops of pre-cum. No surprise, given how long he's been teasing me.

I start to lick the shaft, but Kenneth pulls me back and asks, "Watermelon or mango?"

More fruit? I start to shake my head, ready for kinky time to end and real fucking to begin, but then he holds out his hands. He's got two mini vials of edible lube that must have come from his shirt pocket. Watermelon-flavored or mango.

"Watermelon." I decide I might as well make every fruit salad for the rest of my days remind me of this insane night of hot sex.

Kenneth grins and flicks open the vial. He drips the lube up and down his dick. Then he stares at me and says—with mock seriousness, "What the hell are you waiting for?"

I smile and sink to my knees. I take him in my mouth and am pleasantly surprised by how good the watermelon tastes. It tastes more like real watermelon and less like candy than I expected. I wonder if Kenneth made these lubes himself. Probably.

I hum in appreciation as my mouth slides up and down his dick. My fingers close around the base of his shaft and pump him, getting him harder than ever. I start to go faster. And faster. Until Kenneth yanks at my hair and pulls me back, gasping, "Stop! You're gonna make me come."

I grin. "That's the point."

"Oh no. I'm coming in that pussy." He helps me to my feet and places my hands back on the worktable. I hear the rip of foil and he sheathes himself with a condom.

Then his hand finds my opening and spreads my wetness around before he slowly slides in. Oh my God. It's never felt this good before. I just want him to start pounding. I move my hips, but he places his hands on them, locking me in place. "No. I'm fucking you. Not the other way around, Katie."

He starts to move slowly in and out, leisurely. He doesn't even go balls deep. I'm left panting, mewling, whining, "More. Harder. More."

He doesn't answer. He just puts his hand back on my slit and starts sliding it up and down. It feels good. But I've already come so many times that I need more. "Harder, faster," I whisper again.

He starts to flick my clit. Fuck. "Yes! That! Keep doing that!" I tell him. He complies. He starts to fuck me harder too, holding on tight with one hand as his pelvis smacks into my ass with each thrust. Yes. Yes. Yes. My mind becomes an endless string of yesses as he fucks me. And when I come a final time, it's so intense it's almost painful. It's fire and smoke and a rumbling blast off into space. I float around afterward. Mindless and weightless.

Kenneth comes a second after I do and once he does, his weight presses me into the table for a minute. When his senses recover, he places a small kiss in the middle of my back and says, "Thank you."

"No. That was ... there are no words."

He grins and spins me around. "That good, huh?"

"That good." I agree.

Kenneth disposes of his condom and brings me a warm towel to clean up. Then he dons his clothes. "So, you'd be up for more kinky food sex sometime?"

"Hell fucking yes," I say.

"Good." He smacks my ass and says, "I have to get to work on the morning menu. Competition starts tomorrow. Those guys'll need a lotta options for breakfast."

I nod. I swallow hard. I don't know why, but I'm suddenly disappointed that he's jumping right back to work. He's already scrubbing down our sex table and tossing away the used corn cobs while I dress. I scold myself for being a stupid and needy. We agreed to be fuck buddies. He told me work comes first. I completely agree with that sentiment. Or … at least … I thought I did.

It's just the great sex, I tell myself. I'm used to a mediocre orgasm that quells the urge a bit and that's all. I've never had this kind of crazy sex before. The kind where you just want to bask in the afterglow.

That's it. That's all this is. Just the desire to bask.

But Kenneth's right. I don't have time to bask. I have all the competitions set up for tomorrow.

I head toward the door and Kenneth calls my name.

"Hey Katie, catch!"

I turn just in time to snatch a corn on the cob out of the air.

"In case you want a snack later," he winks.

I laugh and clutch that corn on the cob to my chest. "I'll take good care of it," I promise.

"Nah, make sure it takes good care of *you*." He winks and then walks off into his pantry.

His little flirtation has me floating high again. See? I tell myself. You can totally do this. Casual fuck buddies.

But no casual fuck buddy has made me walk out the door feeling lighter than air.

I toss my corn cob on my minibar countertop, shower off the stickiness, and get rid of my pomegranate seed bracelet. Then I change into a swimsuit, tossing a tank top and shorts over it.

I get Heather and the guys set up on the beach with a bonfire and smore fixings.

The twins heft Heather up on their shoulders and carry her down to the water, splashing through the waves and tossing her in, laughing.

Peter Brown and Jeremiah Bible try throwing marshmallows in one another's mouths. BJ lays back on a towel with his I-don't-give-a-fuck New York Italian vibe.

Heather comes stumbling back up to the beach, soaked,

and Andrew wraps a towel around her. They sink into the sand.

Heather says something. Andrew nods his agreement and gives her shoulder a squeeze, laughing softly. I watch them watching the ocean together. And suddenly, the sense of satisfaction I got from an amazing sex session recedes. I'm left longing again. This time, for something as simple as an arm around my shoulders.

CHAPTER NINETEEN

My watch buzzes. There's no time for emotion in event planning. It's always go-go-go. I've got to go meet with the Cross-Fit person we hired to set up a modified course.

The staff was helping him all afternoon and I have to do a final check to make sure it's not too dangerous. Heather's guys are ripped, that was a pre-requisite for the match-making company, but ... they aren't all Marines or anything.

I walk along the path lined with tropical bushes and trees. It isn't long before I can't see the villas anymore. All I can hear are the night sounds of nature. A bat swoops past, a little too close for comfort, and I duck. Dammit! I shoulda' brought a flashlight, I scold myself.

I hear a voice a little further down. Hopefully, it's the Cross-Fit dude. I round a curve in the path only to stop, dead. It's not the Cross-Fit guy. It's Anthony Drake. He's on the phone. That would be no big deal, except Heather said she gets a weird vibe from him. I slide out of my flip flops and back away silently, so I can hear but not be seen. Maybe he's just closing a real estate deal. Or calling his sister.

"Yeah. Yeah. She's kinky as fuck..."

Not talking to his sister then.

"I'm working on it. God, you're pushy. Well—Rome wasn't built in a day. Yeah. Okay. Well, then, fucking fire me," he growls.

Oh, this is about work. I slink off and give him about twenty more feet. Awkward. How awful would it be if the guy got fired for coming here? Wonder if that's why he's being weird. That would suck. I decide I'll tell Heather about it.

I'm just shooting her a text when Anthony storms past.

I look up and say, "Oh, hi," but he breezes past me without a word. I sigh and wonder if a gift basket is an appropriate 'sorry you got fired' gift. Fuck. Maybe one of those beer of the month clubs would be better. I close my eyes briefly and shake it off. I have competitions to prepare for, male egos to ruin.

I take a deep breath and set off back down the path into the darkness. It's go time.

Go time lasts way too long. The sun rises too fucking

early in the morning. I've gotten maybe three hours of sleep. I drink a crap energy drink. I toss the second into the pocket of my tan shorts. I check myself over in the mirror really quickly as I toss my brown mane in a bun. My blazer and shorts combo rides the line between professional and sexy. I might be showing off a bit today after I woke up and saw my corn cob.

I whistle a little as I toss on mascara, any other makeup will melt off me during the mid-morning challenges outside.

I do a little jog in place to get my blood moving before I toss on my wedges. Today, I don't want to miss a second. The guys know that the group dates are done, and the competition portion of Heather's sorting is up. But ... none of them know what the fuck the competitions will be. I rub my hands together like some evil mastermind as I grab a gift bag and make my way down to the pool area.

Jeremiah Bible gives me a weak, gap-toothed smile and wave as he nurses his coffee.

Peter Brown and Andrew are deep in a conversation about baseball that sounds way too intense for early morning.

BJ stands off to the back, in a corner, watching everyone like he's some kind of bouncer.

The twins both recline in poolside chairs, sunglasses over their eyes. I suspect they're still asleep.

Tony Drake is talking with Heather as I approach. Good. Hopefully, now that she knows work is his issue, they can iron out their little kinks.

I spot Danny coming around the corner with the supplies I need for the first challenge. He agreed to help me last night when he found me running around at three in the morning. I'd thought he was lying ... but there he is. I grin at him and he grins right back. He's kind of sweet when he tells the truth.

I walk over to the edge of the pool and wait for a second until everyone's eyes are on me. "Good morning, gentlemen. Today we'll separate the men from the boys." I raise my eyebrows dramatically. You'll have four separate competitions today. Another two tomorrow. If you survive all of those, then you'll face *the gauntlet*. Are you ready?"

I get a series of nods or quiet affirmations. BJ lazily makes his way closer to the group. Bullshit. They need to get excited.

"I said are you ready?"

Heather waves her hands in the air and yells, "Hell yeah I am!"

The guys chuckle and then start shouting. "Yeah!"

I put a hand to my ear. This is the only time in my life I'm probably ever gonna get to do this. "I can't *hear* you! All together ... are you ready?"

"HELL YEAH!"

I grin as Danny comes to stand next me, a pile of laptops under each of arm.

"Thanks," I whisper.

He just winks.

I turn back to Heather's guys.

"Well, then, now that you're all awake. Let's put those brains to work. You have twenty minutes to buy Heather the perfect gift online. Five-hundred-dollar limit. Your gift cards are in this bag. Choose two day shipping no matter the cost and use the address for the island's PO Box, saved in the document on each laptop's main screen. If you all could line up by that break in the concrete ..." The guys line up as I set the gift bag down by the edge of the pool. I ask Danny to put the laptops down by the edge of the pool. We leave the danger zone.

"Time starts now!" I screech and the seven guys scurry toward the pool. They each grab a laptop and there's nearly a fistfight over the gift card bag before Peter Brown yanks it out of Andrew's hands, grabs a card, and tosses the rest in the pool.

"Foul!" Jeremiah Bible yells.

I simply shrug. "All's fair in love and war."

Six clothed men jump into the pool and dive and wrestle

for the gift cards. I go sit by Heather and Danny follows behind.

Her eyes are locked on the wrestling men in the water. "OMFG. I didn't know wet t-shirt contests worked so well in reverse, but hot damn!" she groans and fans herself as one of the twins gets a gift card, strides out the steps of the pool, yanks off the t-shirt that was clinging to his abs, and reveals wet, sculpted man-torso. He's smooth, so every ridge of his six pack is right there.

Even though he's not my type, I can't help ogling. Danny clears his throat. I ignore him. He scoots closer. I ignore him because the Russian guy just popped the top button of his shorts. And—*whack*—a palm smacks my face and fingers cover my eyes.

"No," Danny growls.

I laugh. "Relax. Geez. Nothing I haven't seen before. Naked Friendships? Remember that?"

"You weren't staring then."

"I'm not staring now," I point at his hand covering my eyes.

"You were going to," he grumbles.

"So?"

"So ... you should let them have their dignity. What the fuck is that?" Danny's rant is cut off. I pry his hand away from my eyes to see what's going on. Of the six guys who went diving, five are now nude. But Russian Twin Number Two is wearing ...

"What is that?" I whisper to Danny.

"No idea."

"It's called the pouch-singlet according to my phone," Heather giggles as she snaps a pic of Rubin or Reval. He's wearing a green swimsuit that basically wraps around one thigh, cups his junk, and leaves way too many pubes visible. It kind of looks like he's attached a very thick green sock puppet to his pelvis. All it needs is googly eyes.

"Goddamn. I feel like I should have a pile of ones next to me," Heather says.

"Why?" I reply. "It's not like they left on anything you could tuck the bills into ..." I shake my head. "Who'd have thought Naked Friendships was so effective."

She shrugs. "When you combine it with naked playtime—"

"Shh." I tell her.

"Yeah, shh," Danny repeats. "My eyes are already burning. I don't need my ears to bleed, too."

I roll my eyes. "You had zero problems with naked men a week ago."

"A week ago you weren't staring at their huevos like you wanted to eat them for breakfast," Danny shoots back.

He's being awfully territorial. I give Heather a 'what the hell' look but only get smug satisfaction in response. She even mouths "harem" at me.

I wave her off. Because that's not happening. I can only handle one fuck buddy at a time. "Ok, new topic. Presents."

She giggles. "So, what do you think they're getting me?"

I shrug. "We'll find out. What do you think they'll get you?"

Her eyes narrow as she studies each of them. "Peter Brown—"

"Butt plugs!" I tease.

She laughs. "Nope. I think he'll get me silk sheets. He made a comment about those the other day."

"The twins?"

"I don't know if they know how to read in English," she admits. "But I don't know if I care."

I chuckle.

"Andrew?"

She turns to me and her smile is soft, different from when she talked about the others. "Well, I'm not sure ..."

"Yes you are."

She bites her lip and shakes her head. "It's stupid."

"Tell me," I growl, leaning in.

"You remember those shoes that were really popular when we were in high school? The ones with the wheels in the heels?"

"Yeah?" I vaguely remember Heather wanting those.

"Your mom would never let us even touch those. And ... anyway, I told him about it. He said he'd had some and he'd teach me sometime."

I hit her shoulder with mine. "That's so super cute! Now I hope he doesn't go buy you a frickin' purse or something!"

She laughs. "I know, right? That would be disappointing. Momma don't want a namebrand bag. Hell no!"

We laugh together and I accidentally end up leaning back against Danny. I glance up at him and he grins.

He says, "I think we should get in on this. I never had those shoes either."

"You didn't?" I ask. "Everyone had them."

He shrugs. "Couldn't twist an ankle. Then I couldn't play tennis." His eyes get dark for a moment and I wonder what he's remembering. Before I can ask, my watch buzzes.

"Time's up!" I jump up and Danny and I collect the laptops and gift cards. I see a lot of sex toy shop websites open. But I also spy a massage. A purse. Andrew's already completely shut down his laptop so I can't sneak a peek.

I put everything on a table nearby. "Alright. Round two. Every good harem member has to be good at making his lady breakfast in bed. You'll have a half hour to complete your task. I'm setting my watch. To the kitchen!"

The guys trot off obediently, ignoring their nudity. Guess they've spent so much naked time on this island, it's no longer a thing.

Danny walks over to me and pulls some suckers out of his pocket. He hands me one and sticks the other in his mouth.

"Where'd you get those?"

"Secret contact."

I narrow my eyes but take a sucker. I'm totally raiding his room again later.

He laughs at the look in my eyes. "It's all hidden."

"Like buried treasure, huh?"

"Yup."

"Maybe I'm a pirate."

"I'd love to see you in a pirate outfit."

I shake my head, about to try to think of something clever to say. But a loud yell breaks up the moment.

"OUT! OUT! NO NAKED MEN IN MY KITCHEN!"

"And that would be Kenneth," Danny says calmly.

I sigh and stride toward the kitchen. If it's not one thing, it's another. I paste on my fake smile and my determination not to let people kill one another.

After a ten-minute break where everyone gets sent to their rooms for a brief timeout like they're three-year-olds, the competition resumes. With clothing. As the guys toss on the aprons and gloves Kenneth has set out, Alec appears in the doorway of the kitchen.

"What the—"

I sidle over to him. "If you're looking for breakfast, the staff just has fruit and toast in the staffroom this morning. The guys are competing today to see who can make the best breakfast."

"Competing for what?"

"What do you mean?"

"What do they win?" Alec asks like I'm a complete and utter moron.

I scowl up at him. "They're getting ranked. Based on how they perform in all the competitions."

He scoffs. "They'll work harder if they get a prize for each one."

"Oh, really?"

Danny slides up behind me and puts an arm around my waist. "That's actually true."

Alec's eyes fly to Danny's arm. And his jaw twitches. He takes a step forward.

Danny drags me back a step, turning me back to face the room, where guys are chopping clumsily. Peter Brown's already cut himself and is getting a band aid from Kenneth's first aid kit. Danny's hand strokes my hip casually.

I mouth at him, "What the fuck?"

He just smiles in response. While I enjoy pissing off Alec, Kenneth is in the damn room, too. And I have an arrangement with Kenneth. I step out of Danny's hold just as Kenneth crosses toward us, heading for a trash can to throw out the used bandage wrappers.

Kenneth winks at me. "Another arrangement?" he nods toward Danny.

My mouth drops open. Oh shit. Oh shit, this is awkward. I need to say something to clear this up. But my mind goes one hundred percent as blank as a white board. As empty-headed as a balloon. I gape like a fish while I just drown in fucking humiliated embarrassment.

A word finally starts to come out my mouth, "No—"

But Danny cuts it off by pulling me further into his side

and saying, "Yup. Just casual, though. She only does fuck buddies."

I'm burning. Literally tied to a pole and set on fire like one of those spinning screaming fireworks. Every single one of my sense is sounding the alarm, blaring, 'Take cover!' and 'Abandon ship!' but my stupid feet are concrete blocks. I'm about to lose the best fuck buddy I've ever had in my life. The most insane, crazy, but best orgasms of my life are about to vanish. Because Kenneth's about to blow up.

Kenneth scans Danny up and down. Then his eyes flicker to me. And back to Danny.

He licks his lips and asks, "You call dibs on tonight?"

Danny grins and pulls me in tighter. "Yup."

To my utter shock and amazement, Kenneth nods. I'm pretty sure a meteor has hit the earth and the apocolypse has happened. I'm pretty sure I've been abducted by aliens and they're experimenting on the synapses in my brain right now. What the fuck? Kenneth is okay with this? Okay with another guy? No, I'm misreading this. Completely misreading—

But Kenneth says, "If you get tonight, then I call tomorrow—"

"No can do," Alec steps in between Kenneth and Danny. He latches onto my upper arm and yanks me out of Danny's grip. I stumble slightly before regaining my balance and staring at him: his buzzed hair, his skin-tight, totally pilot-inappropriate black t-shirt, his army fatigues.

Has he been replaced by aliens too? What the hell is going on here? I've stepped into another dimension.

"If Katie has arrangements with both of you, then she gets to decide what, where, and when. You idiots should leave that up to the lady. But tonight, she's working."

I turn to him and furrow my brow. "I am?"

"Yes," Alec growls. And his gaze gets that intense, heated look we've shared before. "You're gonna tell these idiots," he jerks his head toward Heather's guys, "that whoever wins this cooking challenge gets an individual date."

"I am?" I'm so lost, my brain is just trying to catch up. But the event planner in me spots a giant, gaping hole in his plan. "I don't have a date planned for—"

"Remember the ostracods?" Alec asks.

My eyes widen. He means the vomiting animal thingies? I nod.

"My friend's taking us out on the boat tonight."

"Us?"

"Heather and her date. And you and me. That was the agreement." His tone is gruff, but he's breathing quickly. His eyes are bright. I think he likes the idea that one of the guys might punch him for stealing me away.

I kind of like the idea of the three of them brawling over me, too. My lady parts tighten at the thought.

I look back at the other two. Kenneth's smirking. Danny's pouting. But neither say boo. No fight will be happening. I guess Alec just oozes too much alpha-male to be challenged.

But ... wait.

"I thought you said I get to choose what, where, and when." I narrow my eyes on him. He wants to make rules for Kenneth and Danny but not himself? Asshole.

Alec steps into my space. And sexual energy bites at my lady bits like a little yapping puppy nips at ankles. Non-fucking-stop. Everything about Alec screams, 'I'm gonna take what I want. I'm gonna do what I want. Right now, what I want is to take and do you.' My nipples pebble and I clench my thighs together. Alec gives me a grin. But it's not a happy grin. It's a knowing grin.

"You and I don't have an arrangement. Yet."

He spins around and leaves the room. All the air leaves with him.

Fuck. Who'd have thought one little word would turn my world upside down?

I can't wait until 'yet' happens.

CHAPTER TWENTY

Alec's right. Once Heather's guys hear that they can win an individual date, the big guns come out. What started with fruit parfaits and oatmeal becomes pancakes and 'my grandma's secret seasoned potatoes.' The air gets frenzied.

BJ from Brooklyn smashes his egg too hard and the shell shatters into microscopic pieces inside his bowl. He goes to dump his egg out and grab a new one from the fridge. But there are no more eggs in the fridge. BJ's eyes and mine scan the room to see what the hell's going on.

At the back of the kitchen, I spot the reason. Peter Brown is turning out to be slicker than a greased racoon. The fucker has taken all the eggs left, cracked them, and dumped them into a giant bowl. He's whisking them and whistling. He bites back a grin when BJ realizes where the eggs have gone.

"Sorry bro, making a breakfast casserole."

"You feeding a football team? Gimme a damn egg," BJ demands, getting in Peter's face.

"Whoa, back off. The challenge is to impress Heather, not be a dick," Peter says.

"Only one being a dick here is you," BJ snarls.

Oh shit. The testosterone levels are going nuts. One of them is about to cloud up and rain down hell on the other. And I've got to stop it. Fuck. Next event, I'm hiring a bouncer. I take a step forward.

But then the conflict takes a turn I didn't foresee.

To my right, Jeremiah Bible's meal melts into a horrid mess. He looked up some bell pepper and egg recipe on his phone. I saw the picture: the bell pepper is supposed to act like a pretty red outline and hold the fried eggs inside. Jeremiah's peppers have collapsed, his yolks are punctured, and his creation looks more like a monster that got in a fight and lost a yellow eye.

"Fucking shit!" Jeremiah turns and points a finger at Peter. "You're gonna share those damn eggs or I'm gonna make sure you wear them."

A huge roller-coaster sized wave of discomfort rolls over me. Holy hell. These men are acting crazier than sprayed wasps. And they seem just as likely to sting. I wring my hands. I'm about to call the whole thing off when—

"FUUUUUCK!" A yell has all heads turning to Anthony Drake. Blondie was making waffles. Right now, he's cradling his right hand.

Kenneth runs over with a cool damp towel and wraps it around the burn. He unplugs the waffle iron.

Heather comes by and fusses over Drake, giving him a little kiss to make him feel better, which was probably a mistake.

Andrew gets so distracted watching them kiss that his toast turns black and sets off the fire alarm, which wails like an infant.

Can nothing go right this morning? These aren't even the hard competitions.

I jog over to get a stepstool and put it under the alarm. Only, I'm not tall enough to reach it even with the stepstool. Strong arms come around my waist and hoist me up.

Danny sets me on his right shoulder and climbs the stepstool himself, making it easy for me to reach out and push the button to stop the obnoxious thing. I hold onto him carefully as he climbs back down, and I pretend not to notice the way he drags my body against his. But his eyes catch mine and that blue fire heats my core.

I blush and look away. I don't have time to flirt right now. I need to see if Tony needs to go to the hospital. We're still down the jet for another night or two—so I'll have to get him to a hospital by boat.

Luckily, the burn is pretty minor, and I have some burn cream in my villa.

Before I leave, I tell the guys, "We're going to delay the next two challenges until this afternoon."

Heather interjects. "They're getting delayed because y'all are acting like shitheads. I expect everyone to be better behaved then." She gives them the stink eye.

I fold my fingers together like a schoolteacher well-prac-ticed in scolding. "Otherwise, you will be looking at a plane ride home." I try to sound fierce. I hope I sound fierce. I know I at least make an effort to frown. But the guys are looking so fucking sullen. "Go chill out by the beach for a bit."

"Hey, what about this challenge?" BJ asks. "We haven't finished. Who wins?"

I look to Heather. She walks around from station to station. It's a sad state of affairs. Heather's braver than I am, because she even puts her lips on some of the things they cooked, which look like soggy brown mush.

"Tony wins," she says. His waffles weren't totally burnt, but they definitely didn't look edible. It's a total pity win and everyone knows it. But, considering how awful the rest of the food looks, nobody really has a leg to stand on if they argue. I suppose I should have picked a couple cooks for one or two of the harem candidates. Live and learn.

As the disappointed guys put their dishes in the sink, Kenneth sidles up to me and says, "You let them violate my kitchen."

I lean in and whisper, "I didn't think it would be this bad. I'll make it up to you."

"You'd better."

"I'll let you violate *me* again."

His smile widens and he winks, before he throws a dish-towel over his shoulder like it's an Armani jacket and saunters away.

Heather comes up to me next. "Peter's out." Her tone is clipped because she's so ticked.

I sigh. But, obviously, today has proven Peter not only likes ass, he is one. "I'm gonna get Tony some burn cream and then I'll figure out Peter. We don't have a plane right now. So, I might have to get him on a boat to another island and fly him out commercial or something."

She nods. "Whatever we have to do. But he's gone beyond funny and now he's just a jerk."

"I'll let him know."

"No need. PETER!" she bellows, "Pack your bags! You're a jerk. We don't do jerks in my harem."

Everyone stops and stares at Heather and then at Peter. He glowers, tosses down his bowl of eggs so that they splatter everywhere, and stomps off.

Great. Public humiliation is gonna put him in an awesome mood when I have to discuss logistics. Thanks for that, Heather.

I snag Anthony and lead him back to my villa. Danny tags along. I'm not exactly sure why, unless he thinks Peter might be a jerk to me when I talk to him next. I don't say anything. I'm just grateful for the backup. Especially when he helps me search my boxes for the medical supplies.

We have to dig through six boxes before I can get Mr. Drake some cream and send him on his way, but I do have to let him know, "Unfortunately, our next challenge this afternoon is physical. I'm not sure you'll be able to do it with the burn. I have bandages but still, I don't know if you should risk it."

He just shakes his head. "Had to be my hand. Okay. I'll let you know how I feel."

"Sure thing. And if you need anything, more cream or even if you wanna go get looked at by a doctor, let me know. I can get that all arranged for you."

Danny wanders around my villa as I pack up a couple extra bandages and wraps for Tony Drake. He fiddles with things. And then he turns to me, holding up the corn cob. "What's this?" he asks.

I don't even blush. I go straight to beet-colored. I just shrug and pretend I don't know as I hand Tony a little basket of burn care items. I walk Tony to the door and hold it for him. As he heads down the path, his phone rings. I'm about to head in when I hear him yelling at the phone.

I turn back and hear him say, "That's not what I fucking I sent. I told you what I think the story is. The guy who was trying to buy twenty-thousand tickets!"

He disappears around the corner and I wonder briefly what the hell he's so mad about. Is it work again? Maybe he does have anger issues. I'll watch him tonight on the ostracod date. If my spidey-senses tingle, I'll let Heather know to boot him.

I don't have more than a second to ponder, because Danny's arms wrap around my waist. He leans down until his head rests on my shoulder and asks, "You staring at his ass?"

"No. Don't you always walk people to their door to say goodbye? It's polite."

"Always."

"Lie."

He chuckles, which makes my shoulder shake. "Alright. That was a lie. But, now that I know it's a thing for you, I'll make sure to walk you to the door."

"You don't need to do that."

"I want to do that."

"But, why?" I step forward, out of Danny's hold and onto my porch. I turn to face him. "Why would you want to do that?"

"Because I like you and you like me."

"I'm too old for you."

"Lie."

"I have an arrangement with Kenneth."

"So?"

"So, isn't that like cheating?"

He tilts his head and stares at me. "You're hosting a harem competition. For guys who are cool with sharing a woman."

I point out the obvious. "*You* aren't in the competition."

"But I am a consenting adult—"

"Barely."

He puts his fingers over my lips so he can finish. "And Kenneth and I have come to an understanding."

I narrow my eyes and pull his hands away from my mouth. "Which is?"

"You saw in the kitchen. We'll trade nights." His arms wrap around my lower back and he pulls me in, so our bodies are touching.

The move is very, very distracting. I feel him start to harden against me. And then, somehow, I'm not thinking about how this might be wrong. Or how someone could get hurt this way. I'm staring at the unbelievable blue shade of Danny's eyes. And then I'm guessing at Danny's length as it presses into my stomach. Just over seven inches if I had to bet on it. I lick my lips subconsciously and he smiles.

"So, that's a yes? We're fuck buddies?" he waggles his hips harder against me.

Somehow I resist and pull away. Danny's tropical heat-wave hot. But, he's young. And I feel like I'd be taking advantage. I try an underhanded compliment. "You're too hot for me. You'll lose interest in five seconds."

"Lie again," he grins. "Your tits are bangin'." He eyes them and licks his lips lewdly.

He's ridiculous. But I bite down on laughter so I can attempt to sound disapproving. "That just reinforces my 'too old for you' argument."

He laughs. "I was just trying to piss you off."

"Why?"

He shrugs. "It's cute when you scrunch your nose."

I narrow my eyes and then realize I'm also scrunching my nose. I try to relax, but dammit, years of making an angry face are ingrained. "You need a real relationship. Then you'd realize everything you just said was the worst thing a guy could say."

"I can't have a real relationship."

"Lie."

He shakes his head solemnly. His eyes get a little soft and sad. "Nope. Would you want a real relationship with a guy who's a compulsive liar?" He waits a second, then says, "No one does. They find out and—" he snaps.

Pity surges like a wave through me. "Danny ..." I reach for his hand and grasp it in both of mine. "You're a good guy in spite of that."

He gives me the saddest smile in the world. He looks like those cute puppies at the pound whose eyes grow wide as they watch you walk away, leaving them behind. I always want to adopt all those puppies. Their longing look breaks my heart, because that look says that all they ever wanted was for you to choose them.

Danny's breaking my heart right now.

He uses his thumb to stroke the edge of my hand. After a moment, he says, "It started after I didn't make the team."

I know without him saying the word that he's talking about the compulsion to lie. "The Olympics?"

He nods and stares off at the trees. A parrot squawks and flutters to the ground, then back into the tree again, undecided. I just wait with Danny in silence, respecting his confession, his moment. After a while, he continues, "You want to know a secret? I was relieved. When I didn't make the team, I was relieved."

I hear a crack in his voice that tells me he's being honest. His eyes look wide, a little scared, as they meet mine. I think that might be the first time Danny's said how he really felt out loud.

I hold his gaze a minute, trying to reassure him.

Slowly, it dawns on me why he probably felt relieved. "Your family really wanted you in the Olympics, didn't they?"

He swallows hard and nods. I squeeze his hands. "I'm gonna tell you what Heather told me. What I still struggle with every day. 'It's okay if you aren't who your family wants you to be. You just be you.'"

He bites his lip and looks back out at the trees. His eyes might be the tiniest bit damp.

"Why does she need to tell you that?"

I swallow.

But he told me his secret.

I take a deep breath and rip off the band-aid. "When I was twenty-one, I got pregnant. My boyfriend, Michael, started making all these plans. Wanted to settle down and everything. But ... I lost the baby." I glance down at my feet. I can't maintain eye contact during this next part. My chest tightens. My throat starts to close, and it feels like it's hard to breathe, but I force the words out. "And when I did, I realized I didn't want a family. I don't want to be a mom."

Danny scoops me up into a hug and just presses me into him. Gently. Comfortingly. He just holds me with one arm and smooths his hand down my back with the other.

The tears well up even though I try to swallow them down. I have to clear my throat before I can talk. But when I do, I say, "My family always expected me to get married and stay home. Have babies. It's fucking Oklahoma. That's what you do, right? And I feel like the absolute worst person in the world ... but when I lost that baby, I was ... relieved. I wasn't going to be trapped into that life anymore. At first, my boyfriend said he understood. But one day, I caught him poking holes in his condom."

Danny's hand stops stroking. His arms tighten around me. "When we get back to Tulsa, I'm gonna bury that fucker—"

Fear lances me. "No!" I pull away and stare Danny in the eyes, ignoring my tears. "No. Revenge is a boyfriend thing. I don't do boyfriends. Fuck buddies only. Take it or leave it." I swipe away a tear that's smearing my vision.

Danny's face is clearly at war. I can see how badly he wants to hurt Michael. And part of me rejoices at that. But it also scares me. Because if he can't let it go, I'll have to walk away. And I really, really don't want to walk away.

Danny lets out a growl and picks me up, wrapping my legs around his waist. He holds me tight as he storms inside. He uses his leg to kick the door shut and then he slams me up against it. Then he kisses me, hard. His tongue probes my mouth instantly. There's no soft warm kiss. There's a hot angry tongue fighting with me without words.

Holy shit. Never in my entire life did I think an angry man would be a turn on. But he's not angry at me. He's angry on my behalf. And so, each time he bites my lip or nips my neck I know he's not punishing me. He's wishing he could punish Michael. And protect me. But he's not. Because I asked him not to. A light-headedness that's similar too— yet completely different from—an orgasm fills me. Because Danny cares enough to do what I want. Every nerve ending in my body responds to that feeling and I'm wetter than I've ever been in my life.

That's a good thing, because Danny-the-fuck-buddy takes no prisoners.

His left hand snakes down behind me and grabs my ass, squeezing hard. Then he lifts me up so my feet dangle in the air. He breaks our kiss and stares into my eyes. His are awash with dark fury in a way I've never seen. High voltage hate and lust spark in his eyes. He leans forward so that my body is trapped by his torso and by the hand under my ass. He yanks out a condom and stuffs it between my breasts. Then he yanks down his shorts. He grabs the condom and rolls in onto his length, which is already rock hard. I glance down. Seven inches looks right.

But I hardly get a look before his free hand is back on me. He's rough as he bats at my dress, pulls it up, then he grabs my lacy panties in his fist. He rips them clean off and throws the panties aside. Then he lifts that hand to his mouth and gives his entire palm a single lick. He swipes the moisture over his hard shaft to help dampen the condom. And he stares at me again.

Then he presses the tip of his dick against my opening. He slides up and down along my lips. Once he realizes how wet I am, he shifts his focus to my clit. The hot head of his dick swipes over and over that spot until I start mewling. Then Danny replaces his dick with his hand and roughly starts to flick my bud. He gets a rhythm going, a quick back and forth. The heat builds between my legs. I start to feel drunk. The room starts to go out of focus as everything in the universe becomes concentrated on one tiny spot. There's so much pressure. So much tension. So much emotion. There isn't enough room for it inside of me.

Danny whispers into my ear, "Katie."

My name. That's all it takes for me to explode into heat and light and planets and stars... and love. I scream.

My scream is cut off when Danny smashes into me and

forces his thick dick inside in a single thrust. I cry out, but not in pain. I cry out because the line between fucking and something more is getting blurred. Somehow, even though he's doing exactly what I told him to, Danny smudged that line.

And as I stare into his eyes while he thrusts into me, I realize, I don't think there's any going back.

CHAPTER TWENTY-ONE

Fuck. I ask Danny to leave while I shower. I'm shaken. I don't know what's going on. He didn't do anything wrong. But now I feel vulnerable. Maybe I shouldn't have told him about Michael. Maybe I should have turned him down. My heart cringes at either of those choices. Shit. I realized how attached I am emotionally already. I have no idea what to do about that. I try to shake it off by focusing on work. That's something I can handle. Peter is a problem I can solve.

I find the number for the boat company who ferried Alec over after he had to drop off our jet. I get on the phone with them and then an airline and half an hour later, I've got departure plans set for Peter Brown.

I knock on his door. He doesn't answer. I knock a second time and also try around the back, checking to see if he's used the sliding glass door that opens onto a terrace. Nope. I sigh.

This couldn't be easy, could it?

Fuck.

I go back to the front and knock a final time. Then I use my universal key and open the door. The villa is trashed. The chairs by the small dining table are overturned. He's smashed the glass coffee table. Peter Brown is a sore fucking loser. I take a pic of the room and text it to Heather.

Dodged a bullet, I tell her.

I check the bedroom. Peter's bags are gone. The minibar's been cleaned out. I'm not sure what the fuck his plan is, because we're on a fucking island. Go get drunk and complain to the parrots? There's nothing but this resort. I shake my head and roll my eyes. I figure I better go tell everyone to lock their doors at least until Mr. Pouty Pants is found and evicted. I don't want ten other smashed coffee tables.

I find Heather and the guys down at the beach. A couple of the men are in the water. The twins are running down the beach to burn off steam. Everyone's naked. I don't even bat an eye at all the bojangles bouncing around. Sadly, I don't even want to stare—not because it would make Danny upset, I tell myself—because I've got bigger fish to fry.

I find Heather. She's sprawled out on a towel, using her phone to take a video of the twins. Thankfully, she tosses on a cover up as I approach so that I don't have to stare at her tits. I spent way too many hours when she got her first nipple piercing exposed to them, and probably complained about it enough that she's being decently considerate.

I notice her camera angle has zoomed in to capture the twins from the neck down. "Feeding the cunt monster?" I ask, nodding toward her phone, as I sit next to her.

"You know it," she winks. "Peter gone?"

"About that. Looks like he trashed his villa and ran away."

Heather stares at me a second, processing.

I nod to reassure her it's true.

"What the fuck? Asshole!" Heather springs to her feet and puts her fingers to her lips. Then she lets out an ear-piercing whistle. All the guys turn, as if they've been trained. She waves an arm, calling in the troops.

When I explain to everyone what's happened, BJ jumps to take the lead. He tosses his hand out, karate chop style, emphasizing each part of his sentence with a very distinct chop. "We need to pair off, make sure all the villas are sealed. Then we need to meet up by the pool. We'll do a group search. No ladies are left alone until this bumble fuck's found. Clearly, he's crazy."

"You think he's that bad?" I'm skeptical. Peter's always seemed skeezy—but in a way that made him feel more annoying than threatening. Like those meat salesmen who go door to door. Honestly, I thought Heather would have sent him home long ago. But oral skills … women can be just as deceived by good oral as men can by a good rack. I sigh as my mind brings me back to Peter's villa and the broken table. Clearly, he's no simple meat salesman. Though he did sell Heather on his meat. I blink. I realize I'm fucking exhausted. I'm thinking in shit metaphors about random crap when there's a job to be done. I look up and realize BJ is already leading the team back toward the main buildings.

He's lecturing everyone as we go, "Peter was my room-mate. Thought he was a shoo in. And he has an online poker problem. Or at least, every time I fucking saw him, he was playing."

Heather just narrows her eyes at that information. "So, he looked at me like a fucking pay day?" She tosses her hair. "He's gonna be lucky if I don't punch him in the dick."

We head off toward the main buildings. I warn the staff about the rogue harem candidate and Kenneth and Danny join me in checking all the staff areas. No luck. We get the place locked up and head out as a team. Somehow, I end up in the middle of the guys as we walk down the path.

Everyone else comes back empty-handed, too. Peter's not anywhere in the main part of the resort. Great.

I stare up at the sky and give the universe a sarcastic thank you. It just shit on a stick, called it a lollipop, and shoved it down my throat. Just what I need on an exhausting, emotional-turmoil filled day.

I drag out the energy drink in my pocket and down it because I'm drooping, and apparently Peter was enough of a dick to go hide in the swamp-ass tropical forest. With the spiders and snakes.

I grimace as I swallow the nasty-ass, cough-medicine-flavored drink. Kenneth takes the empty drink cannister from me, tucks it in his pocket, and says, "Next time, if you're tired, ask me and I'll make you some caffè mocha."

"Which is?"

"Basically, hot chocolate with a shot of espresso."

Sold. Shit. I want that every day. Just because. "Call off the search," I joke. "Open the kitchen. That sounds fucking amazing."

Kenneth grins but keeps walking.

On my other side, Danny asks, "What the hell is he thinking? That somehow he's gonna get to stay?"

I shrug.

At the front of the group, BJ shakes his head. "I've seen guys flip out. Bad. When they thought they had something on lock, then lost it." He shakes his head. "Peter's flipped his switch, guarantee it."

Fuck. "Do I call the cops or something?" I ask.

Kenneth shakes his head as he pushes aside a fern. "Nope. Private island. No country claims this one."

I stop dead. I hadn't realized that in my research. The travel agent never said anything about that. "You mean, this island doesn't belong to the U.S. or the U.K. or something?"

He shakes his head.

The realization makes me nervous. "So, there's no laws if he tries to kill us?"

BJ looks over his shoulder at me. His face is grim.

Danny laughs and puts an arm around my shoulder. "Don't scare her man. Geez." To me, he says, "Peter's just pissed."

I nod. But my stomach's still all jacked up on nerves. Or maybe energy drink and nerves combined. I have to clench my fists to stop the shaking. Danny tugs me into his side as we walk, and I try to ignore how much that warms my heart.

We run into Alec on the main path and my jaw nearly drops. My body immediately hums like a magnetic field, crackles like a lightbulb, moans like a porn star.

Danny looks down at me and I realize the moan was out loud. He doesn't look defensive. He just chuckles and releases me from his tight hold.

That only gives me more opportunity to ogle Alec. He

looks like he's been jogging. Unlike the twins, he doesn't jog naked. But he's only wearing sports shorts. Sweat drips down his tanned chest. He has the biggest pecs I've ever seen. Bulky and ripped, they're the size of the huge-ass plate overflowing pancakes at Phil's Diner. And now, thanks to Kenneth, part of me wants to see if Alec tastes just as good with syrup as those pancakes do.

Alec comes to stand right in front of me.

"What's going on?" he asks me, those deep, intense eyes boring holes into my sense of propriety. For a second, I can't remember if it's acceptable to pinch your own nipples in public.

Danny and Kenneth have to explain because I can't. My mouth isn't working. Alec's bare chest is right in front of my eyes. And if I drop my eyes a little, there are abs. Toned, defined, delicious abs. There's one jagged vein that zig-zags down Alec's left side like a lightning bolt. I want to lick it and the droplets of sweat that are trailing down his body. I'm caught up in a lust-filled haze. Thank God we're in a group and that other people can keep their wits about them. Because mine have dried up and blown away like a boll of cotton. All that's left of me is throbbing need.

Fuck. I just had fucking sex with Danny. We're in the middle of a crisis, I tell my stupid horny self. I wrench my eyes away from Alec and force myself to search the foliage for Peter.

My guys update Alec on Peter's stupid stunt. It takes me a second, and then I realize I just mentally called Kenneth and Danny my guys. Fucking shit. Heather's right. I'm already starting to think of them as my harem.

Alec joins the group, nudging Kenneth over so he can walk next to me. A few minutes later, we reach the Cross-Fit obstacle course. It blocks the only path on the island that goes up the mountain. It's the only path leading to a small waterfall and freshwater stream, the only hydration options available on the island for idiots who'd rather pout into the woods than stay at the resort until their ass gets flown back to civilization.

BJ looks over his shoulder at Heather. "Afternoon challenge?"

She nods. "This and an escape room."

I sigh. "Well, there goes that surprise." Not the biggest deal, but now all the guys won't be thrown off by any of the obstacles. That's assuming we find Peter Brown before the competition is supposed to start. We'd better, because I'm gonna be ticked if I have to sweat away my whole day tromping around looking for him.

The guys study the obstacles with interest. The very first one is a mud pit that stretches across the path and fills every available space. It's filled with water so that the competitors will have to jump at the very start of the challenge. The Cross-Fit guy assured me it would make everyone commit better, instead of pussyfooting around the obstacles.

"We need to turn around—" I tell everyone, because that pit is three feet deep and nine feet across. It's not something you could easily jump. It's designed to make sure most people fall in. We need to go back and take a side path—

But Jeremiah says, "I see him!" and points.

Sure enough, Peter is hauling a dripping, mud-covered duffel. His entire body is coverd in sludge from head to toe. He looks like a poop monster.

Heather has the same thought. "You look like a shit that stood up and walked. What the fuck are you doing Peter?"

Peter turns and something glints in his hands.

"Gun!" BJ yells.

Alec's off like a shot. He takes a running leap over the mud pit. He clears it easily, landing on the ground just past it. "Get down," he screams back at us. Kenneth yanks me down into a crouch, but I crane my neck up to watch Alec as he uses one arm to lift himself as he jumps the low walls that are the next set of the course.

Peter sees him coming and startles, turning to run away. But Peter's at a point in the course where there's a cargo net stretching thirty feet into the air. His options are to climb, to try to run around it, or to turn back. He ducks and runs sideways. But I figured most competitors would do that, so the net extends at least twenty feet into the trees on either side, through incredibly thick brush. Peter doesn't make it five feet into the brush before he gives up on that strategy and starts to climb.

Meanwhile, Alec's moved on to the ninja walls. They're six foot 'A-frames' set up on either side of a trench so that competitors have to leap sideways from one to the next, using their feet and their momentum to stay up and avoid a trench below. Alec leaps from one to the next like a fucking pro. He looks like a movie stuntman.

The twins decide they should try and help Alec out. But neither clear the mud pit and we're all sprayed with a volley of brown muck.

They don't stop, however, helping one another climb out of the pit and clumsily following in Alec's wake. On the first ninja wall, Rubin or Revel ends up slipping and sliding on his butt down into the trench, just like a toddler on a slide.

Male pride kicks in with the other competitors. Jeremiah Bible and BJ decide they can't be left behind. They both take running leaps. Jeremiah falls short and his face smacks into the edge of the pit. He falls backward on his ass with a splash.

Andrew argues with Heather about joining them, but she points at Jeremiah saying, "If someone's hurt, they're gonna need you." Andrew helps Jeremiah out of the mud, but the poor man is groaning.

Andrew leads him away down the path. Jeremiah's got a cut on his forehead that's bleeding something fierce, but he says, "I don't need your fucking mothering."

"You need stitches, asshole. I'm not gonna feed you and wipe your ass."

I don't watch them bicker because my eyes are naturally drawn back to Alec. He hits the rope climb section, where a single rope dangles twenty feet in the air. Competitors are supposed to shimmy up to ring a bell. It's the last challenge before the cargo net, which Peter is just topping. Instead of racing past the rope, or climbing it, Alec grabs it and walks backward until the rope is taut. The he runs forward and uses the momentum to launch himself at the cargo net—like motherfucking Tarzan.

My hands fly to my mouth as Alec soars twenty feet through the air.

Next to me Danny pumps a fist in the air like this is a goddamned sporting event. "Yeah!"

Alec lands three quarters of the way up the cargo net and scrambles over the top. He doesn't even attempt to climb down. He jumps sideways and lets himself freefall a bit, before latching back onto the cargo net. He gets about halfway down before he launches himself at Peter, who's ten feet from the ground. Alec grabs onto the other man's torso and wraps him up. He reaches for the metal object in Peter's hand.

They grapple. It looks like Alec might get the gun away.

I let out a breath of relief, until I see him twist the two of them in midair, so that as they fall, Peter's on top and Alec hits the ground first.

CHAPTER TWENTY-TWO

I feel like someone smashed a brick into my chest. I can't breathe. Fuck! Is he dead?

Peter scrambles off Alec and scampers away into the trees. But I don't see Alec move. Shit. Shit. Oh fucking shit.

I run forward but am yanked back. Danny's arms circle my middle. He puts a hand on either of my cheeks. His face is pale, but his tone is steady. "Stay with Kenneth. I'll go get him."

He hands me off to Kenneth, and then takes a running leap over the mud pit. He starts circling around all the obstacles, staying on the ground, unlike Heather's idiots. I try to wrangle out of Kenneth's grip, but he holds firm. That might be a good thing because adrenaline has me shaking like like a Mexican maraca. My insides are all a jumble. And my brain's straight up short circuiting.

Kenneth has to pull my arm a few times before I realize he wants me to move. He pushes his way into the trees, roughly batting away the thick foliage. It's a fight. We have to stomp and shove, and those branches hit back. But Kenneth doesn't stop. He pushes through, and so do I. He leads us in a wide circle around the course.

It feels like it takes forever to get to Alec. By the time we do, Danny has Alec propped up against the cargo net. Alec's blinking and batting away Danny's hand as Danny asks the 'how many fingers' question. Alec looks pale but otherwise alright.

And suddenly I'm pissed. I almost had a goddamned heart attack watching him fall. I pull away from Kenneth and stop a few feet in front of Alec. "What the hell?" I screech at him. "Why the fuck would you run at a guy with a gun?"

Alec lifts his head and his brooding eyes hit me like a bolt to the chest. And I realized I just screamed at him. In public. I just started a fight. I never start fights. His eyes watch me steadily while I process what I've done. The urge to apologize and pacify him nags me like a little girl tugging on her momma's dress. I swat that urge away.

When Alec sees me clench my fists and stand firm, his lip quirks up. It almost looks like he knows what's going on inside my head. But he can't. That's not possible.

Alec answers my question with a casual, "I ran at the guy with the gun so he'd have a target to aim at."

I couldn't be more shocked if some asshole snuck up behind me with an ice bucket challenge right now, dumping that shit all over my damned head. "That is the worst, most idiotic, most awful thing I've ever heard."

Alec shakes his head, then grimaces as if shaking his head hurts. "I scanned all the luggage before I flew anyone out here. If a weapon made it onto the island, then it was my fault."

"Doesn't mean you need to die for it."

He shrugs. "No one else should, though. Besides, it's a non-issue."

"How's it a fucking non-issue! You—"

Danny interrupts, holding something up in the air. "It's a non-issue because Peter didn't have a gun. He had a damn flashlight."

I stare at the long, black metal flashlight in Danny's hand.

My throat gets tight. And for some reason, tears decide to pop up at that moment. I sniff. "A flashlight?" The asshole tears flood my eyes and I look up at the sky to hide them, wiping my eyes like I'm scrubbing at my face in frustration. None of the men say anything. They wait, just watching me. "What the hell was Peter doing, then?"

Alec shrugs. "He just said he can't go back. They'll kill him. Unsure if that was literal or metaphorical."

I bite my lip and shake my head. Then I run a frustrated

hand through my hair. "Alright. Alright. I can figure this out. Can you walk?" I ask Alec.

"Just a concussion, I think," he responds, letting Danny help him to his feet.

"Good. We'll have Andrew check you out and then I'll find a fucker to hack Peter's accounts and shit and figure out what the hell is going on."

One of the twins appears on the other side of the cargo net with a machete. "Stand back," he says. And then he starts hacking away at the net.

Alec clears his throat. "Um ... instead, do you think you can just lift the bottom edge?"

We all turn to stare at him.

Kenneth breaks the silence first. Thank God, because I'm about to jump on Alec and pound him until I give him another concussion. "You can just lift the net?"

"Well, it'll probably take a couple guys but—"

Twin One tosses the machete aside and drops into a squat. He puts his hands on the cargo net and lifts. It comes easily off the ground and he flips his hands so he can power lift it over his head for us.

Alec could have fucking lifted the net. Instead of flying through the air. Instead of doing crazy jumps down the side of the cargo net that made my heart fucking fly into my throat. Instead of falling to what I thought was his fucking death. But what did he do? The idiotic thing. The male thing. The adrenaline-junkie, have-to-prove-my-dick-is-bigger-than-yours thing.

"You're an asshole!" I tell Alec, as I stomp off, weaving my way through the obstacles, guided by Twin Two.

"Don't worry, when she says that, it just means she likes you," Danny tells him.

All the male idiots behind me laugh.

I flip them the bird.

Men. Are. The. Fucking. Worst.

THE HACKER I hire tells me that Peter's racked up nearly thirty thousand in debt while he's been on the island. Seems like he's not only been playing online poker with maxed out credit cards, he called in a loan to a loan shark to put a bet on a horse or something. Something that lost. Guess Peter bet a little too hard on ending up in the harem and Heather bankrolling him.

I roll my eyes and shake my head. No wonder Peter would rather go play George of the Jungle than go home. I scrub a hand over my face and debate whether hiring some cops or private security to boot him off the island is worth it. I mean, he only had a flashlight. Now, he doesn't even have that.

Kenneth and the staff swear he'll come back.

Kenneth's dismissive, "By morning, that idiot will be so full of mosquito bites that he'll be begging us to send him away."

I'm adding to my pro/con list about retrieving Peter when I hear a knock at my door. I set down my notepad, stretch, and pad over to open the door only to find Alec, backlit by the afternoon sun. He's shirtless, but he smells like he's showered, and fuck if the crisp minty scent of his shampoo doesn't make me want to drag my nose down the valley between his abs.

But I remind myself he's an asshole. A show-offy, death-wishy, rejecty asshole.

I glare up at him and cross my arms. "Yes?"

Alec stares at me, reading my mood. When he sees how stiff-backed I am, he leans against the doorframe and sighs. "I'm sorry."

"Sorry for what?" I cock my hip and channel my mother for a quick second before I realize it. Then I exorcise that demon. I do not want to resemble that woman in any way, shape, or form. So, I drop the anger and open the door wider with my patented fake smile. "I mean, come in."

"Don't do that," Alec says, refusing to budge. "You're right to be pissed at me. Okay?"

I cock my eyebrow. "Really?"

He bites his lip as he searches for words. I can tell this isn't easy for him. He doesn't seem like a guy who normally goes around doling out apologies. He's the silent, brooding type. I watch those deep brown eyes of his as he tries to find a way to explain things. The silence draws on. And on.

And it's so uncomfortable. It's like that moment in a conversation right before the other person breaks up with you, that pause in the breeze right before a storm front blows in. I can't stand those moments.

"Just say it," I beg him. Whatever he has to say can't be worse than the million options running through my head right now.

Alec swallows hard. "You know how I said that I've always been an adrenaline junkie?"

I nod. "Today certainly proved your point."

He gives me a grim smile. "Yeah. But, you know what else I said?"

"About wanting more?"

He nods. "I want more, but I *need* that rush."

"I'm confused about how this relates to me."

Alec straightens and the look he gives me burrows straight under my skin. "You're the more."

My very soul faints. That is the last thing I ever expected to hear. It's the absolute strangest, most roundabout compliment I ever received. "I'm the more ... but I'm not what you need?" I'm searching here, trying to understand what the hell he's saying. Because none of this makes sense.

"At first, I didn't think you could be. I mean ... your flight here was your first flight. Ever. I thought you were—"

"Naive?"

"Innocent." He swallows hard. "I didn't know how to handle that."

I narrow my eyes. "Oh, but now that you know I'm up for fucking multiple guys, it's a green light? What the fuck is that?"

He gives a half-shrug. "Kinda. Now I know you can probably give me what I need."

What a self-centered ass. But I'm still dying of curiosity. "What do you mean?"

Alec takes a step closer. His hand reaches out and his fingertips brush my hip. Immediately, my body responds, whether or not my mind wants it to. My libido is one hundred percent on board with whatever Alec needs. My mind is screaming that she's not satisfied, that his apology sucked and we deserve more—my libido clocks my mind in the face and the mouthy, brainy bitch falls to the ground.

I step closer to Alec and his hands dig into my hips. He presses into them, his fingertips curling almost painfully into me. But I don't care about pain. I care about the sense of possession he's radiating. His eyes and hands are raking over me like a fire, branding me as his.

Alec takes a deep breath. "We'll find out if you can give me what I need ... and if we can come to some sort of arrangement, tonight."

Then he steps away. He turns and walks out my door.

"Tonight?" I call out after him.

He doesn't respond. Alpha asshole.

Holy fucking shit, I wonder. What the hell does Alec need? And how the hell can I give it to him?

CHAPTER TWENTY-THREE

Instead of sitting and wondering what the hell is going on with Alec—because, honestly, men's brains are more tangled than a first grader's shoelaces—I check in with Heather and give her my pro/con list.

She throws it on the ground. "Like hell if I'm gonna pay for some search team to go find his ass out there when he did it to himself!"

Andrew is sitting on the couch, magazine in hand. Heather stomps over to sit next to him and he puts an arm around her. He rubs his thumb along her shoulder, and she leans into him. They look homey.

"Don't we have an obligation to help ensure his safety?" Andrew asks softly.

"Not in this situation. He's done fucked himself," Heather crosses her arms. "I can't believe that ass thought I'd just pay all his bills—"

I rub my lips together and brace my arms on the back of the couch. Hurricane Heather's about to unleash.

Once I've weathered the storm and we've all settled on waiting for morning to do anything, I head back to my villa.

Alec's there. He's leaning against the doorway, dressed in black swim trunks with pockets and a white t-shirt. His hands slide out of the pockets and he says, "Where the hell have you been? You have to hurry or we're gonna be late."

"Late?"

"We have to be on that boat for the ostracods in half an hour."

"I thought it was at night."

"We have to take a boat to get there." His look says 'obviously.'

Part of me wants to strangle him. This is very poor planning. People need an itinerary ahead of time!

But the other part of me is so fucking curious about what he needs. It's gotta be something he doesn't think normal sex will provide. We were clearly headed for some sweet vanilla sex on that plane. So, what the hell made him turn tail? My theories are currently wavering between erectile dysfunction and some sort of godawful kink like peeing on people. I googled that on my phone this afternoon. Golden showers. He'd better not 'need' golden showers.

Cause hell-to-the-no. It won't matter that he can get me wetter than the Atlantic. That is plain nasty.

Alec gestures to my door and I realize I've been staring at him. But I do that a lot, so I hope he's used to it at this point. I use my universal keycard and let us both in as I dial Heather's villa and then Anthony's. I let them know the updated timeline.

"You need a bikini and then a longer dress, something that will block the wind, but preferably with a slit," Alec says.

"Okay, that's oddly specific," I toss my notepad and keycard on the table and start to go to my bedroom.

Alec starts to follow me.

I stop. "Um, what are you doing?"

He grins. "What's it look like?"

"It looks like you're trying to sneak a peek at me getting dressed."

Alec just smiles at me and strides ahead. "Oh, I'm not sneaking. I plan to sit on your bed and watch." He holds open the door to my bedroom and gestures for me to enter.

He did not just say that! I cross my arms and stop walking. "Are you crazy?"

"Nope. Come on." He heads into my room and plops down on the lavender comforter, making himself cozy.

I shake my head and walk into the room. "What makes you think I'm gonna agree to get dressed in front of you?"

Alec grins. "Because I'm gonna dare you to do it."

I scoff. "Are we twelve? I'm not intimidated by a dare."

"Ah, but if you do it, I'll tell you the truth about me."

My stomach gives a little ping. My intuition sounds off. My curiosity, which has been prancing all afternoon, turns into a damned bucking stallion. What the fuck does he mean? The truth about him? What's the truth? His tone implies something big. Is he a spy? Some kind of secret agent? Is he in a gang? Is he a contract killer? Or, is it worse than golden showers? Does he have a poop fetish? My hands fly to my mouth when I think of that one.

Holy shit, my mind is getting out of control. And this absolute need to know grows inside me, just sprouts like a weed and takes over, smothering everything else. I have to know. But I need to understand just what I'm getting in return for this little striptease show. I lick my lips and ask, "What do you mean the truth?"

"You do one dare and I'll answer one question. Any question." He reclines against the bed. The position makes me start to think naughty things.

"In full, to my satisfaction?" I ask.

He grins. "If you want to negotiate terms like that, then the dare has to be completed in full to my satisfaction, which will include music and photos and maybe even some very lewd poses."

My entire body turns scarlet. I'm pretty certain even the undersides of my toes are blushing right now. "Never mind," I squeak.

Alec laughs. "Do we have a deal?"

I swallow hard. If he's a contract killer, then I need to know, right? So I can warn Danny and Kenneth and Heather and her guys. Slowly, I nod.

Alec's eyes heat. "Shut the door," he tells me.

Nerves start to rattle my stomach as I shut the door. I have to give myself a pep talk. He's just watching, this isn't actually a strip tease, I tell myself. But, it sure as hell doesn't feel that way. My heart thinks I've been shot out of a cannon over twenty flaming cars. It thinks I'm flying through the air

I take off my short tan jacket and go lay it on the bed, just as I normally would. Alec doesn't move, but I can feel his eyes burning into me and my hands start to tremble as I move them to the hem of my shirt. I pull it off and set it next to the jacket, just like I normally would. I smooth out the wrinkles, because that's what I do, despite the fact that this outfit is going straight to the dirty clothes.

Alec grins when he sees that, but he doesn't say a word.

Next, I pull out my hair and go place the hair tie on my dresser.

On top of my dresser sits a mirror. In the reflection, I can see Alec rubbing himself over his pants as he watches me.

My body clenches just at the sight. Fuck, this attraction between us is strong. The energy in the room crackles like a live wire.

I stay facing the mirror as I unbutton my shorts. I pull them down and bend to pull them off over my heels, so I give him a bit of a show. And then I'm in my underwear. My breasts heave. I'm flushed from the neck up. I slide out of my shoes and then my bra.

Behind me Alec groans. He's watching me in the mirror.

I grow giddy hearing that sound. I get reckless enough to turn around and face him as I lower my white lace panties. I watch him, breathing hard, staring right at the junction of my thighs. I get the panties down and try to kick them at him. They fly up in the air and then down, two feet in front of me. It's an epic fail.

I shrug and start to laugh it off, rolling my eyes for thinking I could be sexy, until I realize he's moved down the bed and clenching and unclenching his hands.

"You'd better put that swimsuit on, or we'll be late." He's gruff.

"I can't rinse off real quick?"

"You just did the goddamned splits kicking off your panties and now you want to rinse off?" he stands and walks toward me. "Get dressed or I'm gonna drag out outside like this and—"

"Okay! Okay!" I hold up a hand. "I was teasing." I really kind of thought that this dare thing was just his way of leading into fucking. Clearly not.

I swallow my disappointment.

Alec stomps over to my drawers and pulls them open, fishing around until he finds a black bikini. He throws it at me. Then he keeps up the search in my closet, yanking dresses out only to examine and reject them.

I come up behind him. "What are you looking for?"

He pulls out a dress that's a white maxi dress with a floral print. It's got a slit right up the middle to my thighs. He shoves the dress at me, eyes raking down my still-nude form. "Wear this one."

I don't even have time to ask why before Alec's out the bedroom door. I scramble into the swimsuit, the dress, and a pair of strappy sandals.

Alec's already waiting by my front door with my phone and keycard in his hands. "Come on." He strides out the door the second he sees me.

"Wait," I run forward, latch the front door and chase after him down the path. When I catch up, I tug on his arm, but that's about as useless as a chocolate teapot. Alec's stacked with muscle and I'm ... me. But I wrap both arms around his forearm and tug, so at least I have his attention. "You owe me a truth!"

Alec stops walking. He takes a deep breath and turns to me. He puts his hands on my shoulders and stares into my eyes. "I know. I'm just trying to figure out which piece to tell you."

"Piece? There are pieces? What the hell, that wasn't the deal! You are supposed to answer my question!"

He nods. "Okay. Ask."

"Why the hell did you run away on the plane?" I can't help the tiny bit of hurt that creeps into my voice as I ask it. But I definitely don't let it show on my face.

Alec bites his lip. His hands slide down my shoulders and caress my upper arms. "Because for the last five years, the only place I've been able to have sex is in a sex club."

"What the fuck?" I have to chase after Alec.

The bomb he just dropped has left me with a concussion. My mind's shaken. When I finally reach Alec, I start peppering him with questions. "What kind of club? Why? When? What kind of things do you do there?"

He shakes his head. "I said I'd answer your question. I did."

"That's not a fucking answer!" I yell just as Heather and Anthony appear on an adjoining path.

Heather's eyes go wide. "Did you get her to yell at you? You're on fire today—first the obstacle course, now this." She holds her hand up for a high five.

Alec reaches out to give her hand a smack, but I grab his

hand and yank down. "You are not high fiving someone over pissing me off."

He just stares down at me, non-plussed. "Yes I am."

He extracts his hand and high fives Heather right in front of me. I grind my teeth together. I want to strangle Alec right now. And not in the sexy way he might be used to at his club. I want to murderize him.

"Y'all have fun on your boat trip," I tell Heather and Anthony. I turn to walk back to my villa.

Alec grabs my arm and pulls me into his side.

For the first time in her entire life, Heather shows some tact, or maybe some pity for me. She and Anthony head down to the pier, where a white boat bobs in the water, leaving Alec and I alone.

Alec bends so his eyes are closer to mine and it's harder for me to avoid his gaze. "I dare you to get on this boat with me," he whispers.

I narrow my eyes. "Not falling for that again."

He shrugs, "Another dare means you get another truth."

My fingers literally flex with the itch to kill him. If I thought I could scratch him to death I would. But the itch to know what the hell he's doing at a sex club is even stronger. I don't know if it's the gossip gene that's embedded on all female chromosomes, or if it's the fact that I secretly hope he's got an unquenchable thirst for pussy. More realistically, he's probably into gags and whips and that kind of shit. I wish I had my phone so I could look it up, but he's tucked it into his pockets.

I glance back and forth between Alec's eyes. "No half-truths this time. I want more than a sentence."

He nods.

I shake my head. "I can't believe I'm doing this." But I turn and walk toward that boat.

ALEC'S FRIEND, Luther, is a nice guy. He's a nerdy, skinny scientist type who's super talkative and super tanned from basically living on his boat and studying these ostracod creatures, which I learn are little and have shells.

"Wait, but how do they puke?" I ask.

"Puke? Who the hell said anything about puking?" Heather turns from her spot on a side bench where she was watching the sunset with Tony.

I bite my lip. She pulls off her sunglasses and her eyes narrow. Then she stands and walks over to me. "I've had a shit day. There'd better not be puking."

Luther cuts in with an awkward throat clear. "It's actually a separate gland that secretes what are commonly called blue tears. It's not vomit."

"Tears?" Heather crosses her arms and stares at me. "What the fuck kinda date are you sending me on?"

I glance over at Alec, who just wears a shit-eating grin. The asshole is absolutely zero help.

"This was arranged the day you put Danny on the plane," I tell her.

She steps into my space, "But, I was right about him, wasn't I?"

"Ladies, ladies," Luther foolishly tries to interject himself between us. "A lot of people claim the mating of the ostracods is one of the most magical experiences of their lives."

"Watching clams puke?" Heather snarls.

Alec and Tony laugh at her choice of words until she turns to glare at them.

Luther says, "Please everyone, just sit down. We're here." He cuts the boat engine. Then he goes to one of the benches and lifts, pulling out snorkeling gear. "Here we go. If you could all put these on."

"Oh, hell no. I'm not swimming in puke," Heather crosses her arms.

I turn and stomp over to Alec, glaring down at him and whispering, "You didn't say anything about swimming."

He looks and me and just raises his brows. "I dare you."

Fucker's gotta lotta nerve. "I'm already on the boat. You already owe me a truth."

"I owe you a truth when you get off the boat."

I punch him. Right in his delicious fucking pec. And it does nothing but make my hand crumple like tinfoil. "Ow!" I sink to the bench seat, cradling my poor hand.

"You okay?" Alec asks.

"You could at least pretend that hurt," I snap.

"Why?"

Luther stares around at all of us, a little frustrated. "You know, professional divers and enthusiasts pay big money to see this. This really is a once in a lifetime thing."

Only Alec stands and puts on flippers and a snorkel mask. And the asshole doesn't even look like an idiot doing it. Why does he have to look sexy doing every-thing? Fuck him and his dark hair and defined chin and his poster-boy body. He walks back over to me and leans down, pulling aside the snorkel's mouthpiece. "Last chance for the dare."

"Why would you tell me this was worse than a donkey sex show?" I grumble.

"I didn't. I just suggested it as an alternative."

"Why?"

"Because I wanted to take you."

Fuck. That makes my insides go all kinds of mushy. They've been doing that a lot lately. I stare at Alec's eyes, which bore into mine despite the goofy headgear.

I bite my lip. Godammit. No guy's ever wanted to take me to some once-in-a-lifetime puking event before. And I'll be damned if it doesn't sound kind of sweet. I scrub my face with my hands. "Dammit all. Fine."

I shake my head. I can't believe I'm doing this. But as I grab Alec's hand and he helps me up, a little thrill runs through me. Particularly when he helps me out of my dress in front of everyone. He reached down and grabs my skirt at the top of the slit near my thighs. The backs of his hands rub gently over my thighs as he bunches the material up and moves his hands around to my back. He squeezes my ass where everyone can't see. I have to work very hard not to react. Because normal Alec is sexy. Seductive Alec is the hottest layer of hell. It's complete and utter torture not to be able to just jump his bones right here and now.

He slowly drags the dress up my back and over my head. Then he throws it aside.

It accidentally hits Luther in the stomach, which I think reminds the scientist he shouldn't be watching. Luther tosses the dress aside like it's a snake about to bite and turns to dig in the snorkeling chest for gear for me, taking the opportunity to adjust himself.

"I can't believe I'm doing this," I say.

From across the boat Heather calls, "I can't believe it either." She looks up at Alec. "You must have a magic wand in your shorts. Because Katie is not the adventurer."

"Hey!" I protest.

She shrugs. "It's true."

Alec laughs as he empties our key cards and phones from his suit pockets and sets them on the bench. "I plan to help her with that."

My heart beats faster. Is that a sex club reference? Is that what he's talking about? Is he planning on taking me to a sex club? Whips and chains and weird costumes and women crawling on the floor in collars run through my head. Then furries, for some reason.

Alec can sense my rising panic, because he takes my hand in his and says, "Hey, it's time." He helps me slide on the flippers and adjusts my mask so it's nice and tight. Unlike him, I don't look good. I look like an awkward duckling stumbling around.

Everything gets better as we get down in the water, which is just chilly enough to perk me up, but not make me shiver.

Luther points to an area off to our left and says, "There."

Where he points, a magical blue glow seems to ride the waves.

When Heather looks over the side of the boat, she gasps. "Changed my mind. Totally swimming in puke."

We tread water while she and Tony toss on flippers and join us. And then we all follow Luther through the water.

We swim through the ocean in the darkness, with only starlight and a distant moon lighting the way. Everything is black and cold and quiet, and the world feels distant. It's an otherworldly experience itself. But it turns completely magical when we get close to the mating ostracods. It looks like an entire galaxy has fallen into the ocean. The waves bubble with tiny, blue glowing stars. The glow extends down and out as far as the eye can see.

Luther's voice breaks the silence. "If you dip your head under and use your snorkel, you can watch the males release the bioluminescent mucus."

Heather says, "So, it's not puke, it's snot?"

Alec says, "Luther, shut up." Then he takes my hand, helps me adjust my snorkel, and we swim together through the most beautiful, fairytale-worthy snot I've ever seen.

CHAPTER TWENTY-FIVE

I'm exhausted by the time we climb back onto Luther's boat. I let Alec help me out of my flippers and yank off my mask.

Luther gives us all towels and we dry off. Then I toss on my dress and grab my keys and phone.

We head back to civilization. All of us are silent, replaying in awe what we just experienced. It really was amazing. I reach for Alec's hand and give it a little squeeze to thank him.

When we get close to our own island, I yawn. I'm ready to turn in. I check my phone out of habit, to see if I've got signal. I see a billion missed calls from my mother and I see at text from my sister.

WTF? Has Heather seen this? Olivia follows her text with a link to a website.

"Lotto Winner Creates Sex Fantasy Island" the article's title proclaims. A big photo of Heather and the guys follows.

Fuck! My hand claps over my mouth inadvertently. Alec leans down to see what's the matter. I open the article. It takes forever to load. I tap my foot impatiently.

Heather asks, "Is everything okay?"

I stop worrying my lip and say, "Just trying to read something my sister sent."

Heather looks at me oddly.

Finally, the damn article loads. And I gasp. I don't even read the first sentence of the article. Because the byline says, by Anthony Drake.

Blinding rage overtakes me and roots me to my spot.

Alec is up and across the boat before I even take a breath. He grabs Drake by the shoulders and yanks him up. "Motherfucker!"

"What the hell—" Heather yells, standing.

I find my legs. I stand and hold the phone out in front of me. "He wrote an article and published it. About your harem."

Heather turns to Anthony Drake. She pries Alec's hands off the man's shoulders. "Is that true?" Her voice is a very deadly calm.

Drake looks wildly around at all of us. Luther hunches farther over the steering wheel, like the drama is too much to handle.

"I told them to write about the guy you cut off in line. The one who was buying thousands of tickets—"

Heather hits him with a right hook. Hard. His face snaps to the side.

She turns to Alec, "Can you throw him overboard?"

Alec nods and scoops Tony up like he's a sack of potatoes.

"Wait! No! Stop!" Tony's protests are cut off as Alec tosses him into the black waves. He surfaces spluttering. "You can't do this!"

Heather looks down at him from the side of the boat. Her eyes glint like daggers. "You're less than half a mile from the island. You can make it back. But then, you can find your own fucking way home."

She turns away.

Luther clears his throat uncomfortably. "Do we at least want to um... give him a life jacket?"

"No!" Heather and Alec growl simultaneously.

They're both furious. I am too, but I know they don't mean it. They just can't see past their anger. I toss a life jacket out into the water and flip Tony the bird.

Needless to say, we arrive back at the island in a fit of

fury. Plans to call Danny's brother the attorney and hack the website and sue the company have been made.

Heather calls all the guys to the pool area and lines them out. "Tony is a motherfucking asshole and if I find out one of you collaborated with him, I will end you! If I find out you are here for anything more than sex and a relationship, I will end you!"

The guys look appropriately cowed because a furious Heather is a sight to see.

"I'm warning you now, I'm hiring a damn hacker to look into all of you. And if I find out anything, you're out!" she yells.

I gently touch her arm. "You might want to tell them what Tony did."

"Oh, yeah."

Once she tells her story, Heather's enveloped in hugs. The guys pass her around, whispering words of affection and reassuring her that they wouldn't betray her.

When she starts to cry in their arms, I take it as my cue to leave. This is their moment to take care of her and build her trust. And when Andrew, my favorite, takes her in his arms, I know she's in good hands.

Alec walks me back to my villa. He stood beside me during the entire pool rampage. And he's silent for about half the walk back. But, as we get away from the other villas and closer to mine, he clears his throat. "So, um, I still owe you that truth."

My stomach tightens. I'd forgotten. With all the chaos and everything with Tony, I'd completely forgotten. I take a deep breath to steady my nerves and ask, "Okay. What kind of sex are you having in sex clubs that you can't have elsewhere?"

Alec grabs my hand and turns to me. We stop walking and I study his face in the moonlight. He swallows hard before he says, "I'm ... an exhibitionist."

Breath whooshes out of me like a whoopee cushion. I even make a squeaking sound. My hands fly to my face. "Oh."

Alec swallows, "I know it's a lot—"

I hit him. "I fucking thought you liked poop sex!"

"What?"

"You're all going on ... dramatic ... drawing shit out ..." I put a hand over my heart. "Motherfucker. Why'd you do that to me?"

Alec stares. "Wait. So ... you're ok with having sex in front of other people?"

"I don't know! I'm just so damned relieved you don't want to poop on me right now. I can't think past that."

Alec laughs and grabs my hand. He starts walking again,

this time twice as fast as we were before. I have to nearly jog to keep up. "Hey, what's the rush?"

Alec stops, suddenly, blocking the path. He leans down and kisses me. And fuck, it's instant waterworks down south. His mouth is hard and hot, and his teeth grab my lip and bite it. When he retreats, I'm breathing hard.

Alec keeps his hold on my hand. He smiles softly and steps aside so we can keep walking. I stop short. There, standing by my door, are Kenneth and Danny.

Alec says, "Katie, I have another dare for you."

CHAPTER TWENTY-SIX

I tremble as I follow him up the path to my villa. My eyes meet Danny's. He gives me a smile and says, "Alec told that if I came over tonight, I'd learn a few things."

I get as red as a pomegranate. I look over at Kenneth, trying to avoid Danny's stifled laughter.

Kenneth doesn't help. He holds up a grapefruit. "In case you're feeling even more adventurous," he winks.

"A grapefruit?" I'm puzzled how he could use a grapefruit on me.

He steps forward and places it in my hands. He leans into my ear and whispers, "It's not for you, it's for me."

Alec grabs Kenneth's shirt and yanks him back. "Let's let her go one step at a time, okay? We don't want to overwhelm her."

My eyes flicker between the three of them. "Why the hell does it feel like the three of you have had some kind of pow-wow?"

"Because we met this afternoon," Kenneth shrugs.

My stomach tightens, nervously. "And what did you decide?"

"We basically decided I get all mornings," Danny said.

"Lie!" Kenneth and Alec say at the same time.

I bite down on a laugh. I turn to Kenneth, anticipating he'll be the most honest.

"Alright, what are the rules? How are we doing this?" I can't believe I'm asking that. I can't believe I'm having this conversation, and this is my life. I'm pretty sure that somewhere on the planet, a pig just grew wings. Because the amazingly impossible has happened.

Kenneth shrugs. "I've never done it before. Besides, aren't you the one with the books on all this stuff?"

Fuck. He's right. What the hell are the fucking rules of a harem? I throw the grapefruit from hand to hand. "Rule one. Lots of sex for the girl. And ass sex is only like a special occasion thing." That's not necessarily true in the books I read, but it's hella true for me. Ass sex sucks ass.

"And group sex?" Danny asks.

For some reason that question tips me over the edge. I was full to bursting with shock and awe and anxiety before but that just tips the scales. Suddenly my brain's tunking over like a tipped cow and my anxiety's jumping up, ready to step in and take over. Fuck. I put my hands on my head. I think I might faint. This is too much. This has gone from exciting to overwhelming.

Alec steps in. "Whoa. Whoa. I think that instead of deciding on rules, we should just kinda wing it."

"I don't wing things," I croak.

"I do," he says. And then he scoops me up over his shoulder and walks me to the door. He uses my universal key, then kicks it open and heads right for my bedroom.

Kenneth and Danny follow, shutting the front door behind them.

Alec tosses me on the bed, and I bounce.

But I'm scared now. And worried. And not at all in the mood.

Until Alec says, "Katie, look at me."

I do, and that magical firefly glow, that instant connection I felt from the moment I saw him, surfaces. He waits, patiently, staring at me, letting the tension build until my entire body is covered in goosebumps.

"You are fucking gorgeous," he growls.

A blush tinges my cheeks.

"Mention her tits," Danny contributes, leaning against the wall, like this is some casual hangout.

"Shut up," Alec grits out.

Kenneth pulls the seat out of my vanity and sits.

Alec gently reaches forward and cups my face. "I want you to change for me again. This time, into lingerie."

My body starts to tremble. I look at all of the guys. And I want to do this for them. But at the same time, I'm scared. This feels big. Because it's not like the fruit thing. That was Kenneth. This is intentional. Doing this will mean I'm saying yes. To this. To them. To all of them.

I stare at Alec and his eyes ground me. I pull up the memory of holding hands with him in the ocean. He wants me to have once-in-a-lifetime things. This is a once-in-a-lifetime thing. "Help me," I whisper.

One side of Alec's delectable mouth twists up in a grin. His big thick hands stroke down the sides of my neck, and over my collarbone. I expect him to slide down the straps of my dress and pull it off me, but he doesn't.

Instead, he extends his hand and helps me off the bed. He has me stand a few feet in front of the foot of the bed and circles me, eye fucking me.

I watch his eyes, but when he circles around back, I sneak glances at Danny and Kenneth. Kenneth is watching patiently, but Danny's already sprung a boner and is covertly adjusting himself.

The idea of all three of them getting off on the sight of me makes me tremble with heat and need.

That's when Alec's hands touch my calves. He squats behind me and slowly slides his palms up my legs. He traces up my inner thighs. His hands hook onto my bikini bottom and he gently drags it down.

My eyes flicker up again. Kenneth no longer looks casual. He's staring at my dress, at the spot where my bikini bottoms used to be.

Alec taps my right foot and then my left, so that I lift my feet and he can get the swimsuit all the way off. Then his hands go back to my calves, making their way back up. This time, his hands take my skirt up with them.

The drag of the material on my skin is sensual. But then Alec's hot mouth bites my ass at the same time. I whimper, closing my eyes for a second.

When I open them, Danny's openly stroking himself through his shorts. Kenneth's breathing hard.

Alec slowly stands behind me, dragging my dress up with him. When the dress reaches my waist and my core is exposed, Kenneth sucks in a breath.

Alec bunches the skirt in one of his hands and then helps me raise my arms in the air. His fingers trace down my triceps before he slowly pulls the dress over my head.

And then I'm standing, in only a bikini top, in front of three men at the same time.

My mind is having trouble registering reality. It's having trouble performing even brainstem functions, like breathing or blinking. Because when Alec circles back around front, I get caught in his dark gaze and forget to breathe.

"Stay here," he commands.

So I do.

Alec goes to my drawers and rifles through for a lacy lingerie top I brought on the off-chance I got lucky on this trip. Little did that scrap of lace know, I'd get triple lucky.

Alec grabs just the lacy bra top and a condom. Then he comes back to stand in front of me, blocking my view of the other men and their view of me as he swaps out my bikini top for the lingerie. He's careful to tweak my nipples before hiding them in the bra cups.

"I thought you wanted them to see," I whisper softly, so only he can hear.

He grins down at me. "I only want them to see what I want them to see."

That sentence is far too complicated right now. My base brain cells do not comprehend. But they do comprehend when Alec circles back behind me. His hands press my thighs until I shift and I'm standing with my legs wide apart.

I hear a buzzing sound start. A vibrator. Pavlovian

response makes my pussy lick her lips. My chest starts to heave. Where the fuck did he get a vibrator?

That thought flies out of my head as Alec presses his tongue to my opening from behind. And that's when I realize he's not just holding a vibrator to me. His hot wet tongue is vibrating against me. He's shoved that vibrator against his tongue, and his tongue onto me.

His throbbing tongue turns my entire pelvis into a hot ocean of carnal sensations. Wave after wave of delicious, scorching hot pulses strum over my most sensitive skin. I've always loved oral. But this is oral on speed. It's more colorful, more intense.

My eyes fly open to watch Danny and Kenneth. They both have their shorts down now, stroking themselves openly as they watch me tremble and shake. Two men are watching me get off. And jerking off to it. Their eyes burn. They wish they were here. They wish they were in Alec's place. But they aren't. And they won't be. Not unless I invite them.

I've never felt so fucking powerful in my entire life. The hot ocean inside me turns into a tsunami. The wet heat slams into my body and I drown in sensation as my orgasm takes over.

"Fuck!"

I'd have collapsed if Alec's hands hadn't flown up and caught me around the waist. He holds me in place and continues to lick, drawing my orgasm out until it's as soft as the rising tide.

I tap his shoulder and somehow, he knows this signals that I'm done.

I breathe like I've just gotten out of the hospital. I feel like I've just had a heart attack. I'm weak, I can hardly stand.

Alec stands up behind me, his hands sliding up my sides and caressing me, even as he holds me steady.

I turn around to look at him and catch him removing a silicone mouthpiece and wiping my wetness from his face.

"What's that?" I ask.

Alec doesn't answer. He clicks a button on the side of the silicone and the vibration stops. He tosses it on the bed.

Then he sits on edge, rolling on his condom and gesturing for me to join him. I walk over and go to straddle him, but he shakes his head.

He turns me back around so that I face Danny and Kenneth. And then he lifts me up like I weigh nothing and slides me down to sit on his dick.

It's so big and hard that it hurts, even though he's given me a mind-blowing orgasm and I'm wetter than a fish in the ocean.

I whimper and he stops. He lifts me up a little more.

Alec whispers, "Put your feet on the bed. Control it."

I set my feet on the edge of the comforter and lift myself up until I'm squatting and he's just inside me. He lets me hold his hands for additional balance and whispers, "Fuck me, Katie."

I've wanted to hear those words from him from the first second I saw him. I slide down his hot shaft and then use my hands and feet to pull up again. I play with just the top half of Alec's dick for a bit, getting used to the sensation.

I watch Kenneth and Danny as I do. Kenneth's got a leisurely stroke going on. He's in it for the long haul. But Danny looks close. And I wonder if I could drive him over the edge. I wonder if I could do that while I fucked another guy.

The thought sends a thrill right through me. It's not the kind of thought I've ever had before. It's as foreign as manners are to a cat. But excited tingles fill me. And I take a second to plan.

I take one of my hands out of Alec's and slide it down to my slit. I circle my clit until I'm moaning again. I make eye contact with Danny.

"You like that?" I ask.

He nods.

"Want me to suck on my fingers?"

He groans. He's almost there. If I push him a little further ...

"Say please," I mutter, bringing my fingers to my lips but refusing to open.

"Please," Danny shudders and starts to spurt.

Fuck! That's hot! I did that. I shove my fingers in my mouth. Then I slam myself all the way down on Alec, getting light-headed as I do. My other hand drifts back to my clit and I close my eyes to finish myself, picturing over and over how I made Danny come.

Alec grabs my hips hard and immediately starts to fuck up into me.

I open my eyes and turn to Kenneth. "Do you like the show?"

"I want to see your rack," he says, as he strokes himself.

I cup my breasts under the lingerie and tease him. "These? You want to see these?"

He nods.

"You'll have to ask Alec, tonight's his night." I reach back and put my arm around Alec's neck.

"Do you want me to show them?"

Alec grunts, fucking me harder. And I'm lost in mindless heat again. Then suddenly, I'm pulled off his dick. He tosses me onto the mattress on my back and rips down my lingerie. Alec yanks off the condom, strokes himself one last time and comes all over my chest.

I grin up at him when I realize what he just did. Alpha asshole.

When he grunts and falls over to the other side of the bed, splayed out, I sit up. I smile at Kenneth as Alec's cum runs down my chest and say, "This what you wanted to see?"

"Come here," Kenneth whispers. I get off the bed and walk over to him. He leans forward and his lips latch onto my cum-covered nipple. And the fact that he's so dirty and naughty makes shivers go down my spine. One of his hands reaches out and touches me. He turns that naughty shiver it into another mini orgasm until I bat his hand away.

I reach down and put my hand around Kenneth's cock. I stroke him. And our eyes meet. I lick my lips and say, "Kenneth, come for me."

He blows his load all over my hand and torso.

I fall into his lap, covered in cum. And he holds me close, pulling my legs in and caressing them.

"Is it possible to die of orgasm overdose?" I ask the room.

"No," all my guys respond simultaneously.

"You sure?" I ask. "Because I think I mightta' died and ended up in *fucking* heaven. Get it?"

They all groan and I laugh.

"I totally googled that joke to tell Heather. But I forgot about it until this very moment."

"You should never google jokes again," Danny says.

I stick my tongue out at him, but he just comes over and grabs my arm. He pulls me out of Kenneth's lap and says, "Let's get you cleaned up, dirty girl."

I wink and skip off to the bathroom, with Danny trailing behind me.

I'm feeling silly and playful and light-hearted as I start the shower. And most of all—hopeful. I don't know how this is gonna work. I have no fucking plan. No fucking clue. But lightning has struck. Heather's won the lotto. And I've won—I glance back to see all three of my guys walk into the bathroom with their eyes on me—I've won something better. Somehow, someway, I ended up with them.

I hold out my hands and say, "I think at least two more can fit in here."

They scramble forward and I laugh. Until I hear a deafening roar outside. My eyes widen. The tropics don't get fucking tornadoes do they? Is it a tsunami? A boat?

I turn to the guys, "What—"

Alec leaps forward and wraps me in his arms, pulling me to the shower floor. "Get down!"

"What is that?" I screech. Fuck my luck—I made a death joke. I shouldn't have made a death joke. Shit. Now a giant wave is gonna crush us.

The guys rush to the window. Then they duck and start whispering. They aren't grabbing me and running. Is it something other than a tsunami? I get up, turn off the shower, and try to peer around them. It's no use. They block the view. And the sound's getting louder.

I run out of the bathroom and into the living room with its wall to wall windows. There, dropping from the sky, is a helicopter. Poised on the edge of the helicopter's open door is a man in a suit. And he's not carrying a damned flashlight like Peter Brown was. He's got a huge mother-fucking gun.

LOTTO TROUBLE: LOTTO LOVE BOOK 2 - PREORDER NOW!

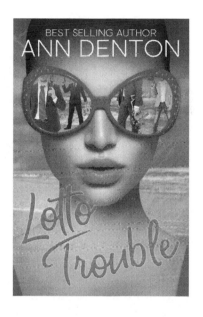

Preorder Available at Amazon.com!

AFTERWORD

Thank you so much for reading! You are amazing, and you are the reason I can keep dreaming up beautiful worlds. If you liked this book, please leave an Amazon review and tell your friends!

Your reviews and recommendations keep me pumped up as I write the next book. So, thanks!

Book 2 of this series is Available for Preorder Here.

ACKNOWLEDGMENTS

A huge thanks to Rob, Raven, Ivy, Coralee, and Thais.

Another HUGE shout-out to all my readers out there. You guys keep me moving and writing! When I see you all chatting about the books in my Facebook group, it totally energizes and encourages me.

MORE BOOKS

My other reverse harem series is the Tangled Crown series. It's a medieval fantasy with a bully romance feel in the first book.

Tangled Crowns Series

Knightfall - Book 1 - Available Here

MidKnight - Book 2 - Available Here

If you liked the sense of humor in this story, you might want to check out my Paranormal Cozy mysteries. They are silly and snarky and full of laughs with a slow burn romance.

The Lyon Fox Mysteries

Magical Murder

Enchanted Execution

Supernatural Sleep

If you're in the mood for more intrigue, check out my Postapocalyptic Thriller series.

Timebend

Melt

Burn

CONNECT AND GET SNEAK PEEKS

If you like to read exclusive snippets from different characters, make predictions with other readers, see my inspiration for books, or just come hang and be yourself, I have a Facebook reader group.

Feel free to join Ann Denton's Reader Group.

ABOUT ME

I have two of the world's cutest children, a crazy dog, and an amazing husband that I drive somewhat insane as I stop in the middle of the hallway, halfway through putting laundry away, picturing a scene.

Made in the USA
San Bernardino, CA
19 February 2020

64637050R00180